GREEN BRIER RIVER

ADVENTURES IN
CINDER BOTTOM **2**

GREEN BRIER RIVER

STEVE VANNOY
AZUL TERRONEZ

Rockrose Press

An imprint of AUTHORS WHO LEAD™

Paperback ISBN: 978-1-968242-00-8
Dust Jacket ISBN: 978-1-968242-02-2
Case Laminate ISBN: 978-1-968242-01-5
eBook ISBN: 978-1-954801-99-8

FIC066000   FICTION / Small Town & Rural
FIC002000   FICTION / Action & Adventure
FIC014080   FICTION / Historical / 20th Century / General

Cover design and typesetting by Kaitlin Barwick
Edited by Lauren Woodbury and Melissa Miller

cinderbottom.com

This book is dedicated to the loving memory of

"SMOKEY" CURTIS VANNOY

and to all those who call West Virginia home.

CHAPTER
1

Smokey lit his last cigarette. He stood in the cool summer morning waiting for Do What to arrive. He had wanted to get up early enough to have some breakfast before heading down the river to fish, but he was running late. He had made it to the bottom of the holler to meet his childhood friend so they could get some quiet time and fish for the weekend.

He was grateful to be spending the day on the river, but his mind drifted back on the troubles he had left behind at home. His grandmother had moved in the month before. Her move had been unexpected, and he hadn't loved the idea of giving up his room. He had only recently inherited the bedroom from his sister. She had moved out, vacating his room, when she married her high school sweetheart. While Smokey thought the man was a donkey of a brother-in-law, he was glad that he had taken his sister away. He would miss her—she was his best friend in many ways—but they had drifted apart ever since she started high school. Her focus had moved outside of the house.

The day was cold, but Smokey was glad the rain had stopped. He wanted nothing more than to relax and enjoy the weekend. He tried not to think about the events of the last week. He and his friend Larry had gotten into trouble. He liked Larry well enough, but that boy could never let things go. For example, when Smokey had called his girlfriend an angry cow, he could not convince Larry that he was just saying what everyone already knew.

His group of friends, the "brothers," as he called them, didn't back him up. Although they had said the same thing about Betty on many occasions, they just didn't have the guts to say it to Larry's face. She was the worst person in Northfork, and everyone—even Larry—knew it. But he had a hard time finding love, and the fact that a popular girl even would give him the time of day, let alone date him, was all that he could focus on. His lifelong friends and their opinions didn't matter—not anymore. Smokey hated that a girl might break up his band of brothers. He was constantly reminding himself that he was stuck in a world that was limited to the confines of the small town he was born in.

Smokey was a tall and wiry kid. He looked older than he was, but his innocent face confused his appearance. He was far from innocent, but he used his charm to his advantage. It was as if his boyish charisma, simple brown wispy hair, and calm demeanor didn't matter. When trouble came, he was always in the middle of it. His dutiful best friend, who was affectionately called Do What, seemed to enjoy his shenanigans. He seemed to long for the next series of trouble that they would encounter.

Smokey was eager for some downtime where he would just throw his fishing line in the water and enjoy a cigarette and a few beers. He never worried about a thing when he was fishing. Today, he was additionally thrilled to be using Do What's brother's canoe so that they could also travel down the river searching for the best spots to catch smallmouth bass. They would camp along the river, build a fire, and chat into the night about the things that sounded important when you were fifteen (cars, women, and how to get out of their small town). Both of their fathers had worked in the coal mines. Do What's father had been injured in the mines and hadn't worked in five years. He spent most of his time drinking and throwing fits of rage. His mother worked a few jobs to make ends meet but they didn't have much.

Do What was one of the smartest guys that Smokey knew, not that his school record would reveal that. He was often the last in his class and was a freshman again because he hadn't earned enough credits to pass to the next grade. Not because he was unintelligent, but because he was often daydreaming and thinking of bigger things than a passed test about the Civil War or geometry. He often contemplated what it meant that we all were alive or whether a man could actually live on the moon. He was a genius if you didn't look at his grades. He was seen as a loser if you talked to his teachers, but Smokey could see beyond the superficial things that those people saw. He saw a brilliant, devoted friend. He knew Do What would stand by him, no matter the personal cost.

Smokey hated school, although he was more successful than Do What. The things they taught in school felt like such a waste of time. He found that the things he learned from Harold the bus driver were far more interesting and valuable. Smokey had elected to take vocational courses in Welch, the biggest town in the area next to Bluefield. He hoped to avoid a life working as a coal miner, even though his father and his father before him had been one.

Smokey had watched his grandfather suffer and die of black lung, and he knew he didn't want that. Black lung was one of the consequences of working in all that coal dust that permeated the air in the underground shafts and tunnels of the mines. The coal miners took black gold from the Earth day in and day out. Years of breathing in all that coal dust left many of those men whose lungs had turned black struggling to keep the breath of life. In the end, they suffered and suffocated, and paid the ultimate price with their lives.

Smokey wanted out. Out of Northfork, out of Welch, out of Cinder Bottom.

He was so eager to be an adult that, at times, he forgot he was still a kid. He had been given a lot of responsibility even though he was the baby of the family, the youngest of five kids. One had already died, two were married, and another was headed off to the army in just a few weeks. He was not eager to grow up, just eager to see the world and get out of Appalachia. Though he hated school, he loved to study. He would read books, study maps, and ask the visitors to Cinder Bottom what the world out there was really like. The tales that he heard intrigued him. He wanted to be part of that world and longed for it to come sooner rather than later.

Smokey realized he had been waiting at the bottom of the holler for nearly forty-five minutes and grew anxious. Do What was usually on time, but Smokey knew that his friend had to convince his brother to let him use the canoe and also give them a ride upriver so Smokey and Do What could make their way down the river to their meetup spot near Hinton by Sunday evening.

Do What's brother, Mike, was usually drunk, and surely this Saturday morning would be no exception. Smokey had hoped that Mike had time to sleep a few hours before having to drive them to the river. He wanted to get the best fishing they could before the late hours of the morning. Do What had promised to do his brother's chores, give him a pack of ciga-rettes, and a pint of moonshine just for him to agree to drive them. Smokey pitched in money for gas, which he had saved for a week from his tips from his paper route.

Smokey had been looking forward to this trip for weeks. As the minutes ticked by, he grew more wor-ried that Mike had passed out after a night of hang-ing at the beer joint and forgot about his promise to drive them. It wouldn't be the first time he let Do What down. One time, he was supposed to pick up Do what from a school field trip in Bluefield, one of the biggest cities in the state, but he was so drunk he had forgotten him. Do What had to hitchhike home and was four hours late.

Mike had been a straight-A student until he was a freshman in high school when his father broke his back in the coal mines. He then had to get a job work-ing in the mines and dropped out of school to help the family. He wasn't the same after that and was often missing for days at a time.

Despite his behavior, Do What always stood up for his brother, even when Mike would beat him. Somehow, Do What could see past Mike's struggles. He saw him for the brother he was before every-thing had changed. However, that didn't alter how Mike acted, and Do What was cautious about trusting him for anything. But since they didn't have a truck,

Smokey had to rely on his friend to get them to the riverhead.

Smokey sat on a log that had fallen on the side of the road. After a while, he lay down and drifted to sleep on the cool spring morning, his bag tucked safely beside him.

He had packed some food, a quilt, and some extra clothes in a plastic bag, to keep them dry in the canoe. He knew that the splashing of the paddles could get his gear wet and didn't want to deal with wet clothes or bedding. He'd also packed a small canteen, a flashlight, a cooking pot, his fishing pole, and a hunting knife he took from his brother's toolbox for cleaning the fish he was certain they would catch.

Smokey loved to fish. He found the quiet and the beauty of the river to be intoxicating. Something about being in nature and alone with the elements seemed to spur on his sense of adventure. He loved cooking over an open fire and having to survive in nature alone with his wit and the elements. He imagined he was Daniel Boone, traversing the wild frontier and living off the land. He had also saved up to buy a pack of cigarettes for the trip, which he figured would last the weekend if he didn't chain smoke.

Do What liked to smoke too but didn't do it if Smokey wasn't around. He wasn't a prude, but he didn't really think of getting things like moonshine and cigarettes. He would buy a comic book before cigarettes and a *National Geographic* before moonshine.

Do What longed to travel to other parts of the world and often daydreamed he was in exotic places like Patagonia or Nepal.

His other friends found his constant droning on about these faraway places a bit of a bore and would often leave him off the list of friends they would invite to hang out unless Smokey was around. Smokey was his best friend and often stuck up for his introverted and somewhat eccentric behavior and tastes.

Do What had grown steadily more invisible at home; his brother was always drunk, and his father often passed out from his daily consumption of a quart of liquor. His mom worked three different jobs at times to make ends meet—doing laundry for miners and often cleaning houses. Do What was a dutiful son, though he seemed to grow more and more reclusive after his father's accident.

Smokey stirred from his brief nap when he heard a running truck off in the distance. He hoped it was Do What. They had to leave soon to make it down the river before all of the fish stopped biting for the day.

He stood, stretching his long limbs and smoothing his hair back down. Smokey was tall for his age and had dark brown wispy hair that was often slicked back with hair balm. He could see the reflection from the early morning sun glinting off the underside of the canoe that was strapped to the bed of the truck.

As the truck approached, Do What hung out the side window, waving his baseball cap in a signal of imminent victory. He had somehow managed to get his brother up and out with the canoe. They pulled over to the side of the road where Smokey stood.

Before the truck fully stopped, the door flung open and Do What hopped out.

"Morning, Smoke," he called.

Smokey gathered his things, flung them in the bed of the pickup, and jumped in after Do What. The cab reeked of liquor. The sheer amount of fumes made it hard to breathe. The aftermath of a long night at the beer joint oozed from Mike's pores. He was not talkative, and that was fine by Smokey. Mike was often harsh and rude when sober but often became passive and somewhat pleasant when he was drunk. The fact that he had been out all night and perhaps hadn't gone to bed yet was probably why he was still in this calm mood.

Smokey and Do What bounced and slid on the bench seat of the truck as Mike took the turns in the road at more than the ideal speed. The canoe wasn't tied down well and was sliding back and forth in the bed of the truck. They weren't worried about the canoe, but the screeching sound it made against the bed of the truck became annoying.

"Smokey, check this out," Do What said. He handed over a copy of an old *National Geographic*. "See there? That's the tallest active volcano in Europe, Stromboli. It's right in the middle of the Mediterranean Sea."

Smokey took the magazine from his friend and glanced at the headline. "Visitors flock to one of the most amazing wonders of the world," it read. He handed it back to Do What.

"That's huge," Smokey said. He was interested, but seeing these exotic places all over the world didn't excite him as much as it made him long for adventure. He wondered what it would be like to sail to that island and hike to the top to see the volcano erupt. He wanted to travel to these places.

However, the more he thought about it, the more depressed he got. As much as he struggled against it, some part of himself believed he was stuck in Northfork and would more than likely always be stuck there.

Do What loved to imagine these amazing places, but never thought he would ever go there. He was intrigued by the history and geography of these places. He knew facts, statistics, and lore of many of the countries and small villages he showed to his friend. The pain of seeing them was more than he could bear sometimes, but he couldn't help himself.

Smokey tried to shake off the feeling and focused on the drive.

The truck hurled down the road at a breakneck speed and arrived at Talcott on the Greenbrier River just as the sun began to peek above the ridge. They wished they would have arrived earlier but were grateful that Mike let them use the canoe and gave them a ride, even if that meant that they had to pay in bribes.

The truck pulled to the side of the road. Mike didn't so much as flinch or offer to help unload the canoe. Instead, once they got their stuff from the truck, he held out his hand for his bounty—the pack of cigarettes and money for his quart of moonshine. Do What handed these over, and Mike sped off back up the road. No words were exchanged, not even a goodbye. Do What waved and his brother gave him the bird followed by the flick of his cigarette out of the truck window. The boys shrugged and gathered their things.

Do What had a small bag and a rolled-up blanket tied with some rope to hold it together. They placed their items in the canoe and raised it up over their heads to carry it down to the river's bank. There was a small fishermen's path that led to the perfect spot to launch the canoe for their adventure. They were both grateful that the canoe survived the winding road and Mike's hectic driving and that they hadn't lost the paddles.

The aluminum canoe was light, but with their clothes, cooking items, and sleeping gear, they had to be careful not to lose their footing as they carried the boat down the small slope to the shore of the river.

There was something calming about the babbling river edge that put them both at ease. They knew they were going to have a peaceful, quiet time on the river—just them, the fish, and relaxation. It was the perfect weekend, and they were ready to go.

They loaded the canoe, and each boy grabbed a paddle. Smokey held the canoe as Do What made his way to the front.

"Walk in the center and hold on to the sides," Smokey called.

The small canoe began to rock side to side as Do What's large, clumsy feet stumbled into the boat.

"Do what?" he hollered back. He nearly capsized the canoe and lost a paddle before steadying his hands on the sides of the small canoe. Smokey smiled as he always did when his friend said, "Do what." The nickname fit and, in fact, Do What thought it was funny too. He was a kind soul and could often be seen helping others when he was in need himself.

Smokey wanted to get out of Northfork, away from McDowell County. He wanted to see the world. He often dreamed of taking Do What to see some of these places but stopped mentioning it to him since he knew that Do What would never leave his mom.

Do What managed to sit down safely and placed his paddle in the water. Smokey raised the back of the canoe and pushed them off the shore. He stepped effortlessly into the canoe and used the back of the handle of the paddle to push the canoe farther into the center of the river.

It was calm and the river flowed gently. The morning sun began to warm their cold faces. The crisp air was refreshing and the quiet sounds of the morning reminded Smokey of why he loved fishing so much. No cars, no noise, and no worries. The river and fishing were the perfect places to get away from it all.

Smokey had a way of attracting trouble. Not that he would go looking for it, but it would find him. He was curious, and that often led to mischief. He certainly didn't run from trouble, but on this trip, he wanted to give trouble a weekend off so he could just relax with his friend.

They didn't have to paddle much to move forward since they were headed with the flow of the river. They just needed to steer and stay in the center away from rocks and the shore. It was peaceful, and they spotted several cardinals. The birds were small, but their beautiful red bodies stood out from the green leaves. They danced in and out of the branches until they eventually disappeared under the canopy of the thick new leaves. In the fall, the color of the leaves made it hard to see them, but the new green growth was a striking contrast to their beautiful feathers.

They paddled for a bit until they arrived at the spot where they wanted to cast their fishing lines. Smokey had already baited his hook with a hellgrammite, a small bug-like animal that looked more like a prehistoric creature rather than an insect. He baited the hooks carefully to avoid the hellgrammite's bite. He hoped that it was enough to catch something for lunch. He prepared the fishing rod for Do What and handed it up to him so they could both fish. They didn't speak much so as not to scare the fish away.

As the sun rose, you could see the small schools of fish come to and from the boat. They were curious. Smokey just hoped they hadn't already eaten their fill of insects. He hoped the fish would bite and that he might get a few nice trout or smallmouth bass, even a catfish or two would make a tasty lunch.

Smokey had first fished in this same spot with his father when he was only eight years old. He had caught many fish there and was certain they would have good luck. He remembered the last time he was there was with his brother, Vernon. He had caught the biggest fish he had ever seen. It was two pounds, and it nearly broke the flimsy rod that his father had ordered from the Sears Catalog. He was proud when that fish fed them all that night. He had a feeling that this spot would bring them luck again.

Do What was not the fisherman that Smokey was. He often splashed his pole into the water when he would drift into thought, or he spoke too loudly and scared the fish, but Smokey enjoyed his company and tolerated the constant questions as much as he could. He had tried to explain to Do What that he had to stay still and quiet, but it seemed as though it would be just minutes before he called out to Smokey to share some facts from his *National Geographic* or turn so swiftly he would shake the boat. The canoe would rock and sway, and Do What would rock and sway as well.

Do What, sometimes oblivious to his size and stature, often tripped over his own feet and stumbled when walking. He was often teased when he was younger because he would walk into walls or trip over rocks. He was always far away, daydreaming, and not focused on what was right in front of him.

Smokey met Do What when he was being teased and Smokey stood up for him. Do What has been loyal ever since, and that happened in elementary school. They spent the summer months having adventures fishing, hunting, and hanging around Cinder Bottom, which was the red-light district of West Virginia, perhaps all of Appalachia. You could find brothels, beer joints, underground gambling, moonshiners, and anything else that most places would deem off-limits. Cinder Bottom drew people in from all over the region. Those who wanted to indulge and not be questioned or troubled came there. It was the ideal location for people-watching and finding some trouble to get into, which Smokey seemed to attract like flies to honey. Smokey was always glad to get some quiet time away from the chaotic Cinder Bottom. He found peace in the fresh air and the water.

In the summer months, the river was a bit lower, which made catching fish a bit easier. It was slow and gentle, which made for a smooth float down the river. Early in the morning, there was still a little chill in the air, so until the sun rose above the tree line, it was cold and Smokey wished he had a cup of coffee. He had brought some to make for breakfast, but the late start meant it was too late to make a fire.

To take away the chill, Smokey lit his cigarette, a Pall Mall. The taste quenched his thirst for coffee and put him into a relaxed state, which is just what he wanted.

He knew that the only time he could smoke was when he was away from home. His pa didn't mind that he drank beer or liquor but didn't want him to smoke. Some of his friends used to tease him that that's how he got his name. "Smoking since birth," they would say to him. The truth was that he was born a blue baby and they didn't know if he would live. One of his pa's friends told his parents his name should be Smokey and that stuck, even though his given name was Curtis. His mother loved that name and used it stubbornly. But Smokey stuck, and everyone else called him that.

Do What would smoke on occasion, but he was prone to daydreaming and often forgot that he had a cigarette hanging from his mouth and wouldn't even smoke it. The lit cigarette would sometimes burn his lip without him ever taking more than a single puff.

Smokey offered him a cigarette, but this time Do What passed, which was fine with him. That meant he could have one more before lunch, which made him smile.

They found the spot where Smokey was certain they'd find calm water and biting fish, but there didn't seem to be as many fish as he remembered from before. He wanted to catch another two-pounder but knew that he would have to be patient if he wanted to catch anything that morning. Smokey was often anxious when he didn't get at least a bite before the sun rose above the trees. He could feel the air warming, and he knew that if they didn't catch something soon, they would have to move to a different spot on the river. They would need to find somewhere shady, a spot where the sun didn't expose the fish, and the fish needed to take a risk on a nibble of hellgrammites.

Do What was so engrossed with his *National Geographic* magazine that he didn't notice the line on his fishing pole begin to bounce. He had a nibble. Then all of a sudden, the pole bent in half and nearly went into the water. Do What was still oblivious until Smokey shouted for him to catch the rod.

Smokey was a little bothered that Do What had a bite and had not even been trying. Do What quickly sprung to life, grabbed the fishing pole, and began to reel it in.

"Don't jerk it. Take it easy!" Smokey shouted. Do What carefully reeled in the line, and Smokey made his way to the middle of the canoe with the net to bring in the haul. Do What pulled and reeled in for what seemed like an eternity as if he was bringing in

Moby Dick himself. The pole bent and wiggled as the fish neared the surface.

"Don't lose him!" Smokey hollered.

"I won't!" Do What called back. The fish made it to the surface and began to thrash. The last yank from Do What's pole sent the fish into the air, headed right for Smokey.

Like catching a fair ball in the outfield, Smokey dove forward and caught the fish in the net.

The boys cheered as if he had just caught the final out of the world series. It was a beautiful bass, probably over a pound and a half. They were both proud and they put it in a bucket of water they had for their prize booty.

Satisfied that they had exhausted the fishing in that spot, they made their way down the river. The sun was shining on the water now. The light danced along the small ripples on the river and made the water sparkle. The morning air began to warm their cold bones, and they found a nice place to pull on shore to enjoy some lunch. They decided to build a small fire and enjoy their catch.

Do What wasn't fond of gutting fish, but Smokey had been taught by his father how to prepare fish, remove the scales, and filet it so they could cook it over the fire. Smokey loved fresh fish, especially when he caught it. He felt a little jealous of Do What, but the grin on Do What's face made those feelings fade. This was the only fish his friend had ever caught. The last time they went fishing, Do What almost caught one of the biggest fish that Smokey had ever seen. He was so distracted with his world atlas that he hadn't even noticed that a fish was on his line. The fish was so big, in fact, that it had leaped from the water with the bait in its mouth. When Do What finally noticed and tried to pull it in, the fish pulled the rod right out of his hand. What had to have been the biggest fish in the Greenbrier River vanished. Smokey had beat himself up for not noticing sooner, wondering if he could have saved the fish. Do What forgot about the whole thing moments after it happened and returned to his reading. For Smokey it was not so easy to forget, but he forgave Do What's lackadaisical behaviors.

Today, he was glad that he was able to help rescue lunch and catch it in the net. Smokey was glad that this day was different.

CHAPTER 2

Once on shore, Do What gathered firewood and kindling while Smokey cleaned and prepared the fish. He fashioned a few green branches together to cook the fish over the open fire. He had learned from his pa to use green branches so they wouldn't catch on fire.

The fire began to crackle and grow, and the boys warmed the morning chill from their bodies. Though it was growing hot in the sun, in the shade it was still cold. The fire was a nice way to warm their hands, and when the flames turned to coals, Smokey used two rocks to position the fish right over the glowing embers. He brought a little salt, which he sprinkled on the fish before setting it in position. The smell of the cooking fish was carried to their nostrils by the whiffs of smoke, and their empty stomachs began to turn with anticipation.

Smokey had packed two day-old biscuits, one apiece, with a little homemade jam that his mother had made from the peaches his aunt had brought up from North Carolina. The biscuit and jam were a welcome treat as they waited for their fish to be done.

Do What, who was always full of questions, thanked Smokey for the biscuits and asked, "Smokey, do you know how far it is to Fish Camp?" Fish Camp was a small spot they could camp for the night along the river. It was often used by fishermen who were looking for a nice place to camp for the night. With the river being so low, it would certainly provide a nice place to rest.

"I guess it's about two miles down the river," Smokey said. He had stayed there many times fishing with his brother but hadn't been there alone. He loved spending summers on the river, but he didn't always have a boat to float down it. He was still surprised that Do What's brother had agreed to lend them the canoe and drive them to the launching spot.

"Do What, how did you convince Mike to let you have the canoe and to give us a ride?" Smokey asked.

"I told him I would do his chores for a month and give him five dollars," Do What said.

"A month?" Smokey stammered. "That's a long time."

"Well, did you want to fish or not? Besides, it's just a month, and it was worth it," Do What replied.

Smokey was always impressed by how generous and self-sacrificing Do What could be. Smokey figured it was because he didn't seem to be bothered much by anything. He didn't seem to hold a grudge or even fight back if he was being harassed, something that Smokey could not tolerate. He hated the way his own brother would tease him and intentionally get him in trouble when they were young. Smokey would never agree to do his brother's chores for a month, no matter what was at stake, not even a ride and a canoe, though he was grateful they had both.

The fish began to crisp, and they took turns pulling off tasty pieces of the cooked flesh, which was as delicious as any fish they had ever eaten. The sun was almost overhead when they finished, and they were getting a bit warm. They doused the fire, cleaned up the remains of the fish, and packed up the canoe. They needed to make their way down the river if they were going to have time to fish and make it to Fish Camp before nightfall.

Once again, Do What made his way to the front of the canoe while Smokey helped keep the canoe steady. Do What lumbered from side to side, rocking the boat, almost tipping it over with every step. Once Smokey had climbed aboard and got settled, he pushed off and the boys made their way down the river. The sun was bright and the heat intense. Occasionally they splashed water on each other to cool down. Smokey enjoyed an afternoon cigarette as much as he enjoyed a morning cigarette, so he took out a lighter, lit one of the Pall Malls, and leaned forward to hand one to Do What.

Smokey had never really liked the way adults treated young people like they didn't understand the ways of the world. He enjoyed hanging out in the Bottom because no one judged him because of his age. They treated him like someone of value. He spent time with Ray at the grocery store. He would go to Big Ma's House in order to help them at the Sunday barbecues. He visited Lorenzo's over at the boarding house to occasionally help clean up or check in a guest. Everyone in Cinder Bottom seemed to appreciate and love Smokey. It made him feel like he belonged to the world—not the world of McDowell County where he lived, but the world that was bigger than him, and that gave him such joy. He longed for times when he could get away, even like this fishing trip because he could imagine himself sailing down the Amazon River or perhaps some uncharted river in a small village.

Do What was just as satisfied to stay home and read comic books as he was to get out on the river, but Smokey felt the desire to go to bigger places. It's not that he didn't love his family, his friends, or even the gentle way that the townspeople of Keystone and Northfork seemed to appreciate the simple things: Sunday picnics, high school football games, and the

Sunday paper. But Smokey wanted to know what else was out in the world. He loved listening to Do What share about the rainforests of Brazil, or the herds of gazelles in the Savanna, and the towering heights of the Himalayas. He knew he wanted to see the world, and just as soon as he could get out of West Virginia he would. His ma would say that he was a dreamer, that he was sometimes too big for his britches, that he needed to come out of the clouds and figure out what he was going to do with his life. Smokey, who had just turned fifteen, thought that he wanted to be a pilot so he could travel the world and explore. He imagined being able to fly to many of the places he and Do What read about and see things that some people only read about. But for now, his weekend escapades to Cinder Bottom, the red-light district, was just as much fun as he could expect to have, and he planned to make the best of it.

They drifted down the river in good time and were nearly halfway to Fish Camp. The fish they had for breakfast was long gone, and their stomachs began to ache for some more food. Smokey had a can of beans, a small loaf of bread, and some coffee as well as a few more snacks such as sunflower seeds and peanuts; enough to last the day, but if they didn't catch another fish before nightfall, they would be hungry for sure.

Smokey found another prime fishing spot, which was situated in the shaded, shallow waters near the edge of the bank of the Greenbrier River. He had fished here before from the shore and imagined how much better it would be with a boat. From the canoe, he was certain they would be able to catch several fish for dinner.

The sun was beginning to dip towards the west, and the calm waters were a perfect place to cast their fishing lines. Smokey baited their poles, and they tossed their lines into the water. Do What returned to one of his magazines, and Smokey laid his head back on the canoe to grab a few moments of rest. He had gotten up early and gone to bed late, which was why he was so sleepy. He had tried to rest the night before, but his excitement about the trip made it hard to sleep. He'd finally started to drift off when he was startled awake again by his brother's friends. They had come home late from the beer joint. He loved his brother, but his friends could be obnoxious, and he didn't like to spend more time around them than he needed to.

Smokey rested the fishing rod between his legs so he could feel if he had a bite. The slow pull of the river kept them moving towards Fish Camp, and the fish were soon to bite for their late afternoon feeding. He figured that since he had just thrown his line into the water, he had a little bit of time before the fish would even bite. In the past, when he fished with his dad, they would often wait three hours before anyone had a single bite. This had taught Smokey to be patient. His dad said, "Smokey, you have to think like a fish if you want to catch one." Smokey wasn't sure he understood what that meant, but he did know that you couldn't be a great fisherman if you were always in a hurry. Unfortunately, Smokey usually was in a hurry.

Today, though, he rested and waited. Once when he was ten years old, he had tried to catch a fish with his bare hands. He'd asked his father, if he could see them, why didn't they just try to grab them and throw them in the boat? Pa didn't discourage him; in fact, he encouraged him to go ahead and try. Smokey stood on the edge of the boat for hours trying to grab a fish that was right in his reach, but he missed every time. He had touched a few but never could grasp them enough to bring one into the boat. His father had explained that the water would bend the light and make it seem like he was grabbing for the fish when in fact they were not where he thought they were. Smokey, being a stubborn boy, didn't listen to his father until he had tried so long that he became exhausted. It wasn't that it was impossible, his dad had explained; it's just that he was misjudging the location of the fish, and that was enough of an advantage for the fish to get away.

Smokey had decided to stick with a fishing pole and bait ever since. He had grown more patient with fishing, but his new patience had not translated to other areas of his life. Smokey drifted to sleep moments after he placed his fishing pole between his legs and closed his eyes. He dreamt of a huge fish and how amazing it was that he had caught more than any of his brothers or pa. He was so proud of himself in his dreams, the feeling of being recognized by his pa for catching the most fish that was ever brought out of the river. He felt his lips turn up with a smile as he drifted further to sleep. He imagined that he was given a prize for the biggest fish caught in the history of Northfork, and a plaque was hung in a town hall with his name on it. They would even name that part of the river after him. *Smokey Bend*, he thought. He imagined a parade and the crowd of people chanting his name, "Smokey, Smokey, Smokey!"

Before he knew what was happening, Do What was shaking him.

"Smokey, Smokey, Smokey!" Do What yelled from the front of the canoe.

Smokey's fishing pole was nearly bent in half and had almost been carried away. He lunged for it and caught it in the nick of time. He grabbed his pole and instinctively began to reel it in, careful not to pull the fish off the hook. He felt the fish pull but couldn't yet spot it in the water. He felt the tension grow as he began to have trouble reeling it in. The line grew more and more taut as he continued to reel the fish in. Do What was cheering and almost dropped his own pole in the water. Smokey stayed focused and didn't pull too hard but kept the tension constant.

"Come to daddy," Smokey whispered. He had watched his father many times coax a beautiful fish from the river.

The line was starting to get harder to reel in and, for a moment, Smokey thought his line might have been caught on the bottom of the river by a rock or branch. He didn't want to lose his hook and weight if he had gotten stuck, though, so he continued to pull gently.

"Do What, paddle in that direction," Smokey whispered. Do What fumbled to reel in his line so he wouldn't drop his pole. The last time the boys had been out fishing, he'd lost his pole and had to jump in to fish it out.

Do What grabbed the oar and paddled in the direction of the fish, helping Smokey to reel in more of the line. The reel was struggling to keep going, so Smokey gave a small yank to see if it was caught on a rock. When nothing happened, he pulled just a little harder. Still nothing.

Smokey stood slowly to see if he could see where his line was. Just then, he felt a hard pull on his line. He pulled back and a beautiful smallmouth bass leaped from the water, just like a whale breaching the waves of the sea. Do What had shown him pictures of gray whales breaching off the coast of California in one of his *National Geographic* magazines. Both Do What and Smokey gasped as they could hardly believe their eyes: it was the biggest fish either of them had ever seen. It twisted and turned in the air as it reentered the water with a huge splash.

The line from his pole continued to pull, and he noticed the line on the rod was beginning to bend. He lowered the pole toward the water and tried to reel it in sideways so he might prevent the line from breaking. He had eight pounds test fishing line on his pole, but with added tension and the weight of the fish, the line was strained and he feared he might lose the fish. Each pull and reel brought the fish closer to the canoe, which was rocking to and fro. It was a miracle that Smokey hadn't fallen overboard as he stood in the canoe. Canoes are unstable if you don't remain low and keep the center of gravity to the keel of the canoe. Smokey was so intent on his fish, that the canoe moved with ease beneath his feet as if it were a water ski gliding on water.

"Gentle there, come on, fish," Smokey said, trying with all his might to will the giant fish into submission. If he didn't catch this fish, no one would believe that the ten-pound smallmouth bass was on his line dragging their canoe down the Greenbrier River. He had only one choice: to catch the fish. If he could catch the fish, he knew that he would be celebrated by his family, friends, and the entire town. They would have to create a special day in his honor, he thought. They would interview him for the paper and maybe even give him the plaque he had dreamed about.

As determined as Smokey was, the fish fought just as hard. It pulled and twisted in the water, fighting to get away. With Do What paddling in the direction of the fish, Smokey was able to draw the fish closer with each tug. But Smokey could feel his reel begin to grow sluggish like the line was getting twisted as he reeled in. He didn't have time to worry, he just kept steady pressure on the line.

The fish decided to change directions, and Smokey directed Do What to change course and keep the fish in front of them. They were now headed back upriver and towards some small rapids. The rapids were big enough to capsize the canoe, but were shallow enough that the fish might get away. Smokey needed to act fast or the fish would be lost for sure. He began to reel the fish in a bit faster and with a little more force. With each turn of the reel, the fish pulled even harder, nearly knocking Smokey to his knees. Smokey sat so that he would remain in the boat instead of falling into the river.

"Come on fish, just relax," Smokey said. He wanted this fish more than he ever wanted anything in his life. If he could catch it, he'd be so proud. He would be a legend and everyone would probably cheer his name. He would give Do What credit as well; after all, he was the one that secured the boat and got them a ride to the head of the river. They would both be famous, and he could smell victory.

At that moment, the fish leaped out of the water right near the boat. He hollered to Do What to get the net that was under the seat. Though they hadn't seen anyone on the water for hours, suddenly there was a small flat-bottom boat with two boys, just a little older than Smokey and Do What, headed in their direction. When the fish leaped out of the water, the two boys in the other boat whooped and hollered.

"Go get 'em!" they cheered as they watched the fish splash near their canoe. Smokey continued to reel in his line as the onlooker boat made its way closer to their canoe. Do What tugged for the net a second time and the rocking nearly sent Smokey headfirst into the water.

"Be careful!" Smokey shouted. With that, Do What tugged one last time and the canoe swayed and lunged and sent Smokey headfirst into the water. Luckily, it was only up to his chest, so he flailed for only a moment before he realized he could stand. He got on his feet and continued to reel in the fish.

The two boys continued to get closer and cheer Smokey on.

"Come on now, get it, you stupid idiot!" the taller of the two boys yelled. He was dirty, like he'd been rolling in the dirt, and he was missing at least a tooth or two.

The boys looked like they were Do What and Smokey's age by the stature of their bodies, but their faces were darkened by the sun. As Smokey's pa used to say, they looked like they were ridden hard and put away wet, like two cheap stable horses who lost a race. Their boat was so close to theirs it almost collided with them. The older-looking boy in the other boat had a cigarette in his mouth and a fishing pole in his hand. The younger boy was rowing the small boat towards them.

Smokey knew that he had only one chance to get the fish before it disappeared into the rocks of the small rapids ahead. He decided to give the pole and reel one final hard yank to bring the fish in.

He took a deep breath, gave a hard heave, and he reeled the rod with all his might. The giant fish leaped into the air at that precise moment and the last pull sent the fish sailing in the air over Smokey's head. It was so huge it looked like a small plane flying overhead.

When the fish was just over him, Smokey saw the fishing line snap. He tried to dive towards the fish, but it was moving too fast and too far for him to reach it. The fish sailed in the air.

Do What freed the net and tried to dive toward the fish's direction to recover their prize fish. The fish hit the side of the other boys' boat, and the taller one reached into the water and seized the fish. He had it in his net. They all cheered. It was a fishing miracle. The fish was so big it nearly knocked the boy right out of the boat. Smokey began to wade towards the boys.

They high-fived each other, and Smokey reached them with a smile. "Nice catch!" Smokey said.

The boys were still celebrating and didn't pay any attention to Smokey, who was nearly at their boat now. Do What managed to get the paddle he had lost in all of the commotion and pulled up beside Smokey and the small boat.

"Thanks for saving my fish," Smokey said.

"Your fish?" the older boy said. "It looks like it's my fish, doesn't it?"

Smokey smiled and reached out his hand.

"Thanks again, but can you hand over my fish?" Smokey said.

They lowered the still flailing fish into the boat. It bounced and flapped. They had no intention of giving up the fish.

"I'm the one that caught the fish right out of the air, didn't I? Wayne saw it all." Hans said. He was taller than his younger brother, Wayne, by nearly a head. He was lean, and his muscles shone through his white T-shirt.

"Yeah, that's right, Hans caught it in mid-air," Wayne said with a lisp.

"Now you boys saw me catch that fish, so it's mine," Smokey said. Water dripped down his face, and his nostrils began to flare. "Give me back my fish," he said.

"It ain't your fish, it's mine! It's in my boat, in my net, so it's mine," Hans said. He stood with the cigarette still hanging from his mouth. He took a long drag and then flicked it at Smokey. "What are you gonna do about it?"

Hans stood in the boat, which made him seem like a giant from Smokey's point of view. Smokey wasn't going to let these two hooligans take his fish, not the one that was supposed to make him famous. Do What had his hand on the side of the boys' boat to keep the canoe from drifting down the river without Smokey. Smokey was angry now and made his way closer to the boat.

"I'm gonna take my fish, that's what I'm gonna do," Smokey said. He was now close enough to reach the side of the boat. He pushed off from the bottom of the river and tried to jump high enough out of the water to reach the fish, but Hans pushed the fish in the net to the other side of the boat.

"You ain't takin' my fish," Hans said. He aimed his fishing pole in Smokey's face. "Don't make another move."

"What are you going to do? Cast your line in my direction?" Smokey said. He snickered at the attempt to intimidate him with a three-dollar fishing pole.

Hans didn't hesitate and removed his hunting knife from his waist holder and aimed it at Smokey.

"No, I'm gonna gut you like a pig," Hans said with a calloused hiss.

Smokey let go of the side of the boat as Hans lunged for him in the water. Smokey wished he had the knife that was in the bottom of his canoe. At least he would have a blade to protect himself with; in the water, he felt vulnerable. Hans lunged at him again but stumbled slightly and almost fell backward.

Do What grabbed a hold of the boat and rocked it side to side. He rocked it so hard that both boys went sailing into the water. The knife was tossed into the rapids and the fish, net, and all leaped out of the boat.

"The damn fish is getting away!" Hans yelled.

"Get in the boat, Wayne. Let's go get it!" Hans said. Hans was trying to find his knife, but it was lost in the rocks of the small rapids. The fish and net could be seen making their way down the river. Both boys jumped back in the boat and started to follow the fish.

Hans turned back to scowl at Smokey and Do What. "I'm gonna get you two, mark my words." Hans and Wayne began to chase after the fish headed downriver.

Do What and Smokey were no match for the rowboat. They would never catch up to the boys, nor would they ever catch the fish. It hadn't become the largest fish in the Greenbrier River by being stupid; it knew how to survive, and it had managed to escape once again. It was as if it had caused the ruckus and freed itself from its captors.

CHAPTER 3

Smokey beached the canoe on the side of the riverbank and helped Do What get out. He was impressed with Do What's quick thinking to dump the two boys out of the boat. He was certain he could have taken the older boy in a face-to-face fistfight, but a knife fight in the water was a different story.

"Thanks for the save," Smokey said. He took off his wet T-shirt and wrung out as much water as he could.

"No problem, buddy. You'd do the same," Do What replied. He wasn't a violent guy. He would rather take a beating from his brother than defend himself violently. But his strong sense of loyalty meant he could never stand by and see someone he cared about get hurt.

"I can't believe they stole our damn fish!" Smokey exclaimed, taking off his jeans and wringing them out. He looked silly dripping on the shore in his underwear and sneakers, but he was so mad he almost didn't notice, until a small group of kids who were on the other side of the river skipping rocks started to point and laugh. Smokey scowled at the boys and sat on a rock to warm in the sun, fuming from anger. It was as if his anger was causing the steam rather than the sunshine. He thought for a moment that perhaps the fish got away and was still close by, that they could catch it again, but he knew better. Still, he hung his head low into his chest, fighting back the tears of anger that welled up.

"Stupid fish," Smokey said. "I'm gonna kill those boys." He knew he had no intention of actually killing them, but he was so mad that he was glad they weren't close by. He went into the canoe to grab his knife and held it tight in his hands. No one would believe he or Do What had caught a ten-pound bass. They would tease and laugh at them, and that made him fume even more.

They stayed just long enough for Smokey to stop shivering and put on his semi-dry clothes so they could head down the river to make it to Fish Camp. They were behind schedule by about an hour. At this rate, they wouldn't make it before sundown.

They loaded up the canoe, and Smokey pushed them off as usual into the middle of the river so they could begin to paddle. He had lost the will to fish for the rest of the afternoon. No fish would ever compare. He wished he had brought the fish into the boat before the boys came, he wished he had a do-over so he could show off his prize catch, but now all he had was a lost fishing hook and the biggest fish tale in southern West Virginia.

Smokey knew they needed to fish if they wanted to have something for dinner besides the few provisions they brought with them, but his heart wasn't into it. The boat meandered back and forth as his mind fixated on his lost fish. He scanned the water, hoping for any sign of the fish, but there was no trace of it. Do What cast his line into the water, letting the line troll behind them. He cast the line out and reeled it in methodically. He had almost given up when, with a sudden jerk, the pole bent.

"I got something!" Do What shouted. Smokey barely raised his head to see the pole bending towards the water.

"Reel it in slowly," Smokey said in an even voice. He watched the pole bounce while Do What reeled in the line. There was no sign of struggle, it wasn't snagged, but something was still bending the pole. Do What kept a steady pace, and he could tell by the drag that whatever was on its line was nearly at the canoe. With one big tug, the pole yanked to the surface the net that had once held the prized fish. The hook and broken fishing line were still embedded in the netting.

Do What brought the net aboard, his shoulders slumped with a sigh. At least Smokey could retrieve his hook, and they had an extra net now. Smokey smiled when he saw the line and hook and knew the fish had probably survived many such attempts to catch it. He was the largest fish in the river for a reason. He was lucky, and that made him worth his weight in gold.

Smokey picked up his pole and placed the hook back on. He baited it and cast the line back into the water. He knew that as the sun was beginning to set, the fish would come out to feed. They might still have a chance to catch at least a small fish for dinner.

It was only a matter of half an hour before both Do What and Smokey had caught two fish. Smokey caught a decent size trout, and Do What caught an equal size catfish. They put their poles away and started to paddle. There were a few small rapids near Fish Camp that made it difficult to maneuver in the dark, so they hurried as much as their tired arms would allow.

Just before dusk, the boys made it to the beginning of the rapids. They had just enough light to maneuver through the small rapids safely. They made it to the soft sandy beach of Fish Camp, pulled the canoe ashore, and began to make camp. Smokey gathered firewood to build a fire, and Do What took the supplies and provisions out of the canoe.

Do What lifted the plastic bags out of the canoe that contained all their belongings. The bags felt heavy and hard to lift. He managed, with difficulty, to get one onshore. When he went to sling the next over his shoulder, he realized why they were so heavy. Water began to drain down his back and into his pants and shoes. Both bags, meant to keep their gear dry, had filled with water. His heart sinking, he realized there must have been holes in the bags or that they had opened up during their scuffle with the two boys.

He quickly dropped the bags and called over to Smokey. They both stared at the waterlogged blankets and wet clothes. There was no way that the blankets or clothes would dry before bed. Smokey's clothes were still damp from falling into the river hours before.

They took some rope they had packed and fashioned a drying line close to the fire. They hung the wet blankets and clothes and began to prepare dinner. Smokey was glad to see that the food he had packed was still dry. The cigarettes, too, were dry. They had been in his tackle box along with his fishing gear, knife, and lighter.

They cleaned and prepared the fish and created a woven snowshoe grill to turn the fish evenly over the fire. The smell of the cooking fish made their stomachs crave the warm, fresh fillets. They split a biscuit and waited for their fish to cook.

The night sky was filled with stars, so many that they seemed like a blanket of twinkling lights hanging in the night. They both stared in quiet contemplation as their fish roasted. When it was ready, they feasted on their catch. If they still had the huge fish from earlier that day, they might still be hungry. They would have saved it to show off when they returned home the next day. But they didn't dwell on that because they didn't want to slip back into the painful moment that they lost it.

When they had eaten their fill, they sat back and each enjoyed a Pall Mall. The night was beginning to turn chilly, but they kept the fire burning and had plenty of firewood for the night.

The warm coals burned down to a steady glow. If they kept the fire stoked, they would keep warm enough for the night. The late spring and early summer months were cool along the river, but there was no sign of rain, so they rested at ease.

In the distance, they could hear faint sounds coming from just down the river. They couldn't quite make out what it was, but they could see a small flickering light. Smokey remembered that there was an old cabin, used by youth groups and such during the late summer that usually sat empty this time of year. It was a small cabin with a covered porch and small campfire ring outside.

As the night wore on, the noise grew louder. Soon, they were able to make out some music; a fiddle or perhaps a banjo was playing. Smokey wanted to know what was going on. He motioned for Do What to get up and follow him down the river bank a short way to see if they could make out who was in the old cabin.

They followed a small but clear trail that fishermen used and made it down the river with relative ease. The moon cast a strong enough light that they were able to see pretty well once their eyes were adjusted to the darkness away from their campfire. When they were directly across from the cabin, they could see into the window that was lit with a small lantern and a few candles. The sound of the music was familiar to Smokey, who had heard bluegrass music most of his life. There was some hollering and stomping they could make out. They couldn't see faces, but they could tell there were probably four or five people in the cabin.

The door to the cabin opened, and the sound of the music filled the air until the door was closed again, muffling the music. In the light, they saw what appeared to be two people on the porch.

At first the figures were obscured by the night, but when they lit a cigarette, the boys could see their faces plain as day: it was Hans and his brother, Wayne, the two boys who stole their fish. They stood on the porch and puffed long drags of their cigarettes, which glowed in the darkness. With each deep inhale, the embers illuminated their faces.

Smokey's blood began to boil again. He wanted to leap across the river and beat the night out of both of 'em, especially the tall one, Hans. He was the one who had taunted him while he was in the water. He noticed where the other boys had tied their boat to a small dock on the shore near the cabin. He despised seeing it and wanted nothing more than to sink it. He turned to Do What.

"Do you see that?" Smokey said. "Those are the boys that stole our fish."

"I see them alright, damn fools," Do What said. He wanted to take a drag off his cigarette but didn't want to attract attention to their location.

Smokey wasn't satisfied with just standing there. He wanted to know what these boys were doing in the cabin. Did they have permission to be there? Were they squatting in the old place? He had seen other people stay there on occasion, but for the most part, it stayed abandoned most of the time.

Smokey wanted to get a better look, so he pointed to a tree and told Do What to give him a boost. Do What obliged and hoisted Smokey on his back until he could reach the first limb. From that vantage point, he was able to see the men who were playing music inside and the boys who were now putting out their cigarettes.

Smokey reached for a higher limb. He heard a crack as the limb snapped under his weight. The branch crashed into the water, and he nearly fell in after it.

Hans and Wayne turned and looked towards the sound. Do What ducked and hid in the bushes, and

Smokey stayed perfectly still. The boys glanced and glared in their direction, but eventually they went back into the cabin.

Smokey and Do What sighed with relief and made their way back to their camp.

The fire was nearly out when they returned, but they managed to stoke the embers to bring the flames back to life. Smokey was still damp from his river escapades and shivered in the night chill. He wished that his bag hadn't leaked and that he had a nice, warm blanket to sleep in. Instead, he shivered and hated those boys even more.

Do What was getting the remainder of the provisions out of the canoe when he noticed two small plastic air mattresses.

"Hey, Smokey, what are these?" he asked. With all of the commotion with losing the fish and setting up camp, Smokey had forgotten the air mattresses he had tucked into the bottom of the boat. He had won them as a prize for selling the most subscriptions to the paper route he had. He was grateful that at least they could blow up the mattresses and not have to sleep on the hard ground. It would be cold but more comfortable for sure.

They blew up the air mattresses and laid on them, feeling as comfortable as if they were on a fancy sofa in an expensive hotel.

"This is nice," Do What said. And he meant it. His bed at home was nothing more than a pallet of blankets on the floor in the living room. He used to share the bedroom with his brother, but had been kicked out when he was twelve. He had grown accustomed to sleeping on the floor.

They rested by the fire and enjoyed another cigarette. The music from the cabin continued into the night as a faint but ever-present noise. Smokey hated the idea of those boys being just up the river, the ones who stole his fish, celebrating and carrying on. He wanted to get back at them. But how?

He had an idea.

"Do What, come on, let's go," Smokey declared. He stood up and grabbed the paddles and headed to the canoe.

Do What didn't question him, just picked up a paddle and followed.

Smokey directed Do What to get in the front of the boat as he pushed them off the sandy shore, down the river towards the cabin. The light of the cabin grew brighter and the music louder, and they made their way to the other side of the river, staying close to the bank so they wouldn't be seen. They drew closer to the cabin and the dock. Smokey pointed to the shallow opening near the rear of the cabin. The reeds of the river hid them from the sight of the cabin. The marshy waters were slow-moving there, and they could get a better look inside.

They could now make out the faces in the cabin. They could tell that the others were also boys about their age. They must have snuck into the cabin. That wasn't hard; Smokey had done it many times. He never thought of staying inside, since it was so visible from the river. The boys got the canoe secured on the shore and snuck around to the back of the cabin so they could peek inside to see what they were up to.

From the back windows, they could see the boys had all kinds of trash and empty beer cans strewn every which way. They seemed to be alone—no adults, just a bunch of boys crashing a cabin for the night. At first, it seemed like a harmless night of music and drinking. But then they saw something that surprised them.

In the corner of the main room, there was a boy tied up to a chair, blindfolded. He had blond hair and seemed to be just a few years younger than they were. With most of his face covered, it was hard to make out just how old he was, but he seemed to have bruises and a few cuts near his temple. Who was this boy and why was he tied up?

Smokey had to get a better look. He instructed Do What to follow him to the other side where there was a window. Maybe the boy was in trouble and needed help. Smokey already hated the two boys and figured that the company they kept couldn't be much better.

When they got to the side window, they could see the boy more clearly. They could see that he had been crying. Streaks of tears had made trails through the dirt on his cheeks. Smokey wondered what they had done to him. Was this their twisted sense of fun?

Smokey tried to get up higher above the window ledge so he could see the other boys. Do What offered to boost him up on his back to get a clearer view. He peered over the ledge of the window, moving slow and careful.

There were a total of four boys, the two they had already met and two others who seemed cut from the same cloth. They were in dirty clothes, and all seemed a bit older than he was by a year or two. They seemed familiar, but Smokey couldn't place where he might know them. They were stumbling a bit, playing their instruments sloppier and sloppier. Their rhythm was slipping. Judging by the number of beer cans and empty mason jars, which had no doubt held moonshine, they were starting to get drunk and a bit rowdy.

"Do What, we gotta help that boy," Smokey whispered as he lowered himself down to the ground.

"How we gonna get him free?" Do what asked.

Smokey had begun to form a plan while making his way back to the canoe.

"Follow me," he said.

They followed the small path back to the river. Smokey figured the boys would continue to drink until they passed out, or at least he hoped so. He and Do What would go back to camp and get everything prepared. They would rest a bit and pack up their gear. Once the drunken boys were asleep, they would make their way back to the cabin to untie and get the captive boy out. They had been drinking, so he hoped that once Hans and the others were asleep, they would stay that way for the night.

Smokey hoped that whatever they had planned to do with the tied-up boy wouldn't happen until morning. Maybe it was just a prank or some sort of hazing, but he didn't want to take a chance. He knew they had to get the boy free no matter what.

Do What was ready for anything, so the plan sounded good to him. He rarely said no in the first place, so a chance to get back at the boys who stole their fish seemed like a good idea.

They laid on their air mattresses, both listening intently for the faint sound of the banjo that played softly and drifted over the river. It had a calming effect on them, and just for a minute, they forgot there was anything to be bothered with at all. They stoked the fire just enough to keep their hands warm, but they were careful not to let it flare up into too bright of a flame. They were far enough up the bend of the river that their camp wouldn't be visible from the cabin, but it didn't hurt to be cautious.

They were grateful they had the mattresses to rest on instead of the hard ground. Though they tried to fight sleep, the music from the cabin stretched out into the night. Eventually, they both drifted off, sound asleep.

The cool air kept the side of their bodies that was away from the fire chilled, and the warm glow of the fire brought them both comfort as they slept. They slept peacefully until, suddenly, they were awoken by the loud sound of a hiss. Smokey leapt from his mattress, trying to find what he thought was a snake. The hissing seemed to continue but there was no sign of it anywhere.

Do What started to snicker, then erupted into a full belly laugh.

Smokey stared, confused, looking for what might be the source of his amusement but saw nothing. Then he noticed that the air mattress was flat. A hot ember must have popped out of the fire and onto his mattress, melting a hole small enough to create the hiss. They both laughed hard and then remembered that their voices might carry so they brought it down to a dull roar. It was what they needed, a laugh.

They soon realized that they both had fallen asleep and had no idea what time it was. They stopped and listened. The music was gone. No glow came from the direction of the cabin. The boys must have passed out. This was their chance to get to the cabin before the boys woke up. They hoped that the captured boy would cooperate when they came to get him free.

The moon was still high in the sky, which lit the calm moving river that seemed to dance in the night. The boys packed up the rest of their gear and extinguished the fire before making their way to the canoe.

Smokey steadied the canoe, and Do What made his way to the bow of the boat. He had finally made it without rocking the canoe. Smokey pushed them off the shore, and they glided towards the cabin from Fish Camp.

CHAPTER
4

The moon was a perfect guide, the bright reflection leading the way to the cabin. The river, though low and seemingly calm, moved more swiftly than they had experienced before. There were larger rapids ahead, and the current was growing steadily stronger, so they didn't have to paddle much to pull them closer to the cabin.

They slowly brought the boat to a stop and placed their paddles on the shore to steady themselves. They sat quietly, watching to see if there was any sign of the boys. When there seemed to be no movement from the cabin, they carefully disembarked.

They dragged the canoe to the shore and gathered some grass and weeds to try to disguise it. It was dark near the cabin. The trees covered them and provided shade from the moon. It was perfect cover for them as they crept closer to the window.

They approached the side of the cabin where the boy was when they last saw him. Do What bent over and allowed Smokey to climb on his back. Smokey stretched his way up so he could peek inside.

He saw the four brothers passed out on the floor along with the beer cans and banjos that had been littered across the room. The boy they had come to rescue was still tied to the chair, though now he was slumped over. He must have passed out too, tired from trying to wiggle his way free without any success.

Smokey glanced around the room to identify the best way to sneak the boy out. He frowned as he saw that the only way in or out of the cabin was through the front door.

Smokey signaled for Do What to let him down. He described in a whisper what he saw. They needed to get the captive boy's attention without waking the others so that they could signal to him they were there to help. His mouth was still gagged with a handkerchief, but the blindfold had slid down from his eyes. Smokey wished that he had a flashlight. He could shine the light in the boy's eyes to try to startle him awake, but it had been in the same plastic bag that his sleeping gear was in. It was back at camp, waterlogged and useless.

Do What had the idea to make the mating call of a hoot owl, which might make enough noise to wake the boy without disturbing the others. If the others did wake, he hoped they would just assume it was an owl. Smokey was skeptical, but how else would they communicate to the boy that they were there to help him? The last thing they wanted was to scare him and wake his captors. They were running out of time and options, so Smokey agreed to try Do What's crazy idea.

They found an old stump near the outdoor fire ring that the other boys had been using as a stool. Smokey dragged it beneath the window and climbed on top. Once he was in position, standing steadily atop the log, he signaled for Do What to start hooting. Do What had been studying the hoot owl since he was eight years old and could imitate their cry as good as any old owl could do. He had even won the all-county bird calling competition when he was in sixth grade.

Smokey stood in position and Do What started to hoot. Smokey watched the boy and waited to see if he would open his eyes. Do What stopped and looked at Smokey for approval. Smokey gave him the signal to keep on going so he did, just a bit louder this time.

The moon was shining just right into the window so that he could see the boy's position well. He had on shorts, sneakers, and a T-shirt. He didn't look like he was expecting this abduction by the way he was dressed.

With the louder hoot, the boy lifted his head and, with a dazed look, blinked as he tried to focus his eyes. He had slouched down in his sleep, and the rope was digging into his wrists, which were tied behind his back. At first, Smokey thought that he was going to fall back to sleep, but the next loud hoot jarred him awake. Smokey waved his hands to get his attention. He didn't want to startle him, but they only had so much time before Do What's hooting woke up one of the other boys.

The boy stared in Smokey's direction, but he seemed confused. The moonlight behind Smokey was blinding the boy's vision after waking from such a deep sleep.

Smokey continued to wave his hands and signaled for Do What to stop hooting. The boy cocked his head, trying to make out what Smokey was communicating. Smokey was using his best charades to tell the boy that they were there to help. Smokey gestured toward the front door. The boy seemed confused by the waving hands and pointing and shrugged.

Hans shifted on the floor and made a long groan. The captive boy's eyes widened with fear as Smokey crouched down to avoid being seen. When he peeked over the window's ledge, the captive boy was looking back at him, and Hans had fallen back to sleep.

Now the captive boy was trying to use his head to communicate. Smokey held up his hands to signal for him to wait and then pointed to the front door again. The boy seemed to understand and nodded in agreement. Smokey and Do What made their way to the front porch to see if the door was unlocked. They hadn't thought about that nor what they would to do if it was locked.

They stepped onto the porch, and the boards croaked like a bullfrog. They stopped in their tracks, feeling the boards with their feet to find a quieter path. The cabin was old, and the boards were worn from years of families walking to and from the river.

They made it to the front door, and Smokey checked the doorknob to see if it was unlocked. He slowly turned the knob and the door creaked open. He whispered to Do What to follow the plan. Do What headed off the porch and around the other side of the cabin.

Smokey slowly opened the door. There were some small patches of light coming from the window, but it was otherwise dark and hard to see. He didn't want to trip or kick over an empty beer can.

The captive boy was now wide awake and staring at Smokey. He seemed to be trying to tell Smokey something, but Smokey couldn't quite make out what. He took another step forward, and the boy's eyes alerted Smokey that something was wrong. Smokey felt a hard blow to the back of his head and the lights went out.

Smokey woke up with a splitting pain in the back of his skull. He felt like he had been tossed from the bed of a truck. His body ached and his head pounded. He must have fallen asleep at Fish Camp. Maybe he had been dreaming about the boy at the cabin and his attempt to rescue him. He felt relieved that it was just a dream.

But as his senses returned, he realized he was not at Fish Camp. He was in the cabin. And he was tied to a chair. The boy he was supposed to rescue was still tied up across from him. He looked even more terrified than when Smokey was sneaking into the cabin to free him.

The group of brothers surrounded Smokey's chair, glaring at him.

"Yeah, that's one of them, the one that stole our fish," Wayne said.

Wayne was talking to Frank, his oldest brother. Frank was tall and muscular, and a bit more put together than his younger brothers. He had brownish blond hair, which was cut short and clean, and the chain around his neck looked like the ones that held dog tags, the ones soldiers wear to identify them if they die in battle.

Frank stood right in front of Smokey and glared at him from head to toe.

"He ain't nothin'," Frank said. He began to circle Smokey's chair, watching his every move to see how he might react.

Smokey, still a bit dazed from the blow to the head, tried to focus long enough to scan the room, but his eyes were blurry, and he had a hard time lifting his head. His hands were tied behind his back, and his mouth was covered with a rag. Smokey was still disoriented and thought he was seeing double-vision when he spotted Mickey, Wayne's identical twin.

The captive boy, who was tied up across from him, looked weary and his eyes were welling up in tears. His childish face made Smokey think he was probably twelve or thirteen years old. He shivered in the night air, but it wasn't just from the cold. He seemed genuinely terrified.

Smokey slowly regained his focus, just as Hans burst into the cabin and marched toward Smokey.

"Where is he?" Hans demanded.

Smokey stared at Hans in silence. He knew he was asking about Do What, but he gave no indication that he had anything to say.

Hans drew closer and repeated himself. "I said, where is he?"

Smokey tried to speak, but the rag muffled his words. Hans pulled down the rag that was covering his mouth. He struck Smokey across the back of his head with his open hand, and he winced. Smokey acted like he was deprived of oxygen, heaving and gasping for air. Hans stared at Smokey agitated.

"I said, where is he?" Hans repeated.

Smokey sat up, took a long breath, and looked directly at Hans. He whispered in a low tone words that were unrecognizable. Hans took a step towards Smokey.

"I'm not going to ask again. Where is he?"

Smokey looked him dead in the eyes, cleared his throat, and said, "He went home to screw your mother some more."

With that remark, Hans slugged Smokey hard in the stomach. He coughed and spit as he tried to recover the air that had been pushed out of his body. The younger boy shuddered and closed his eyes. He was trembling now and started to cry quietly.

Wayne turned to the kid and said, "Oh, are you gonna cry now, little baby?" He began to slap the back of his head to antagonize him. The kid began to cry even more. He tried to hold back the tears, but it was as if the dam had been broken and he couldn't stop them. He went from a gentle sob to full on crying within seconds. Wayne teased him more and slapped him in the face a few times, laughing and snickering at his display of tears.

Frank tapped the shoulder of his younger brother to signal him to stop. Wayne retreated and Frank stepped toward Smokey.

"So where is your friend, the one from the river?" Frank asked.

Smokey stared at him but said nothing. He had dealt with boys like this all his life. He had watched them intimidate and humiliate younger boys, and he was sick of it. He had been toughened up over the years because his older brother and his friends had teased and picked on him a lot growing up.

He stared into Frank's eyes, and he recognized something familiar about him but couldn't make out why. His tall muscular build and strong commanding presence seemed out of place for a McDowell County boy, but Smokey figured that his military training had smoothed over the unrefined demeanor that his brothers still possessed. Smokey said nothing and stared at Frank.

Frank took a closer step towards Smokey and bent over to look him in the eyes. "I guess you like to learn the hard way," he said. Frank slapped Smokey with the back of his hand so hard that the chair flipped over backwards. Smokey hit the ground hard and his lip began to bleed. The other boy was sobbing but Wayne had tied another rag over his mouth to quiet his tearful song. Smokey reeled from the pain, but he didn't attempt to get up or move.

Frank stood over him and glared down.

Smokey looked up at him and said, "I forgot to tell you I wasn't ticklish." He glared right back at him.

The anger began to rise in Frank's face, but otherwise he didn't react. He turned and walked towards the door where Mickey, the twin with the paddle, stood.

"Watch them," Frank said and signaled for the other boys to follow him. They left the cabin and filed out the door, spreading out to find Do What.

Mickey felt emboldened by the power that was bestowed on him to watch over the prisoners. He smacked the paddle into the palm of his hand and stared at the two tied-up boys, one weeping in his chair and the other sprawled backwards on the floor. The night air was cool and, though they had lit a lantern, the cabin was a darkened mess. The room was littered with the evidence of a night of rowdy fun.

Mickey kicked Smokey and pointed at him with the paddle. "Don't try anything or I'll have to bash your head in," he said.

His wispy hair and dirty overalls made him seem older, but you could tell by his eyes that he was no more than thirteen or fourteen. Smokey thought that he recognized him. He seemed familiar like his older brother, but Smokey still couldn't make out why.

Mickey danced around the chairs, taunting them. Smokey watched him and measured each move. When Mickey stood still, you could see his leg shaking, like he was nervous, but he tried to cover his nerves by chanting names and teasing them with his paddle, telling them they were gonna get it for sure and that they would find their friend.

Smokey glanced at the other kid and noticed he had stopped crying but was still shaking from his previous bout of tears. The boy seemed delicate and out of place. Smokey had been around boys like Hans his whole life, but this boy seemed like he was not from Cinder Bottom, Northfork, or anywhere in between. He wondered why they had taken him captive and wanted to get information from Mickey now that he was in charge of guarding them.

"So, you are the lackey, the one that gets to do the dirty work?" Smokey said. He watched as Mickey tensed up. He made his way toward Smokey, raising the paddle over his head.

"What did you say, little boy?" Mickey said. Smokey tried to rock his chair right side up so he could make eye contact with him.

"You're the guard, the one that's given the dirty work. Let me guess, you do the chores no one wants? Do they make you stay behind often?" Smokey knew this would get under his skin. He had finally rocked his chair to a position where he could push himself up.

Mickey made his way to Smokey, pulled his chair up on all four legs, and held the paddle to his face.

"You shut up," he said. His nostrils were flaring, yet his legs were still shaking.

"You like to fish?" Smokey asked, hoping to get the boy talking. He saw a small glare in his eyes but didn't respond. He tried another question. "You play baseball?" Smokey asked, staring at the paddle. By the way the boy was holding it, he seemed like he knew his way around a baseball field.

Mickey nodded but didn't say a word.

"I played for my school team last year," Smokey said. He noticed Mickey relaxing some, but he still seemed cautious. "I play second base. What about you?"

Mickey stared at Smokey, uncertain if he should respond. He glanced back to the shivering boy, then back to Smokey. "Left field," he said hitting the paddle at his feet as he stared at the floor.

"You look like you might be a good hitter. The way you hold the paddle, I can tell." Behind his back, Smokey worked his wrists back and forth, trying to loosen the ropes.

Mickey pretended to swing at a fastball.

"Hit the winning home run the last game," he said proudly. His shoulders seemed to relax a bit more. Smokey glanced over at the kid and noticed him making eye contact with him. He seemed to be trying to signal him, but Smokey couldn't make out what he was telling him.

He turned his focus back to Mickey.

"A home run, huh?" he said. He felt the ropes loosen enough to slide his right hand free. Smokey continued to talk and keep Mickey at ease while he tried to figure out what the kid was trying to signal him about.

After a moment of subtly casting his eyes around the cabin, he spotted Do What glaring into the window behind Mickey, who was now chatting freely about his baseball triumphs. If Do What could divert Mickey's attention, Smokey would be able to free himself and the other boy. He didn't hear the older thugs anymore, but he guessed they only had minutes before they returned.

Smokey nodded slightly to Do What, who ducked down and made the hoot owl mating call loud beneath the window. Mickey turned toward the window, putting his back to the boys.

Smokey took his chance and sprang from his chair, tackling Mickey to the floor. The younger captive stared in awe while Smokey wrestled the paddle out of Mickey's hands and pulled his arms behind his back. Mickey squealed and Smokey covered his mouth and stared into his eyes.

"Don't make another sound," he threatened.

Do What burst in and grabbed the paddle just as Mickey stood upright again. He raised the paddle behind his shoulder and wound up his upper body to deliver a home-run hit straight into Mickey's gut. Mickey yelped and fell to the ground with a thud.

Smokey used his loosened ropes to tie Mickey up while Do What freed the other boy. Smokey finished tying Mickey's hands and legs behind his back and shoved the rag into his mouth. Mickey wasn't seriously harmed, but the blow had been enough to scare him out of fighting back.

"You okay?" Smokey asked, turning to the object of their rescue attempt.

The boy nodded.

Smokey signaled for Do What to see if the coast was clear. The brothers would be returning soon, and they needed to get out of there.

Do What nodded and the three boys slipped away out of the cabin and into the night.

They hurried to the brush along the riverbank. The kid followed like a lost puppy. He didn't speak but he whimpered continuously under his breath. By this point in the night, the moon had set behind the mountains. The night was dark with only faint starlight to light their way. Just as the boys reached cover, they heard Frank and the brothers return to the cabin. They were too far away now to hear the exact words the boys were shouting, but their cursing and anger were obvious even at a distance. The boys didn't waste any time and headed straight for the canoe they had hidden. As usual, Smokey held it steady while Do What made his way to the bow. The kid followed behind him and sat in the middle. The boat rocked back and forth beneath his unsteady feet.

"Hang on to the sides of the canoe," Smokey whispered. He pushed and they made their way into the middle of the river. They paddled quickly, careful not to splash the oars in the water. They didn't want to attract attention to their whereabouts. They sat still and focused as they paddled stealthily past the boys who were now searching the shoreline.

"You little asses better come out! We'll find you!" Hans shouted.

The canoe had to float past the cabin on their way downstream. The boys all held their breath as they passed, desperately hoping they would go unnoticed.

Smokey and Do What paddled in unison and carefully followed the current of the river. Do What kept an eye out for rocks that might wreck them or alert the others of their whereabouts.

Smokey could see in the starlight how afraid their new companion was. He was shaking and trembling. He seemed even smaller now and frailer than when they first spotted him through the window in the cabin. Smokey wondered how he came to be in the hands of these obviously ruthless boys. He wondered what had brought them together and why they had kept him tied up. They were almost past the cabin when one of the boys shouted.

"There they are!" Frank held a flashlight in their direction, lighting up the river.

Do What and Smokey paddled more vigorously, hoping to get out of range of the boys.

The angry mob stood on the shore, shouting and goading the boys in the canoe. They launched rocks in their direction, each rock splashing closer and closer to the canoe.

"Get the boat!" Frank yelled. The brothers headed to the flat-bottom rowboat that had easily sped away from them before.

Do What and Smokey paddled as fast as they could, careful not to fill the canoe with water, but each stroke brought more of the river into the boat.

Smokey kept looking back at the bigger boys. He trembled with the thought that they might catch them. The river grew rougher with each stroke. The current was becoming more intense. They had to be careful if they wanted to avoid becoming a twisted heap of aluminum at the bottom of the river. But the rowboat was gaining on them, and Smokey knew they needed to move.

CHAPTER 5

"Faster!" Smokey shouted. He and Do What pulled in unison, making the canoe glide like a swan on the river.

Hans and the other boys were paddling hard and beginning to close the gap between the rowboat and the canoe.

But as the pursuers made it to the center of the river, their boat started to slow. The rowboat was taking on water. The boys were continuing to paddle, but each stroke sank the rowboat farther into the water. The boat finally dipped under the surface and sank, sending the boys splashing into the water.

Do What grinned at Smokey. While Smokey was in the cabin, he had pulled the drain plug from the rowboat. He had known that the boat would be fine until all of those boys got into it and started paddling. Once the waterline reached the drain hole, each pull of the oars had sunk the boat further and further.

Do What and Smokey raised their paddles in a brief moment of victory.

They paddled slower now, grateful to have escaped. The boys couldn't catch them now. They sighed in relief and relaxed as each passing moment took them further from the mob of rowdy boys and the cabin.

"Are you alright?" Smokey asked, turning to the kid, who nodded. "What's your name?"

The boy looked more relaxed now, but he was shivering—probably from the cold, but they didn't have a blanket or a dry coat to offer him.

"Martin Brent Ferguson III," the kid said, trying not to let his teeth chatter. "My friends call me Brent."

"Nice to meet you, Brent," Do What chimed in. "So, how did you end up with those guys?" he asked, shouting over his shoulder.

Brent stared up at Do What, not certain how to answer. He hesitated.

"I was taken from my school by those boys," he finally said. He seemed to return to the moment when it occurred as he described what happened.

He had stayed after school to do his homework and finish his violin lesson. He usually waited for his nanny to pick him up when he was supposed to stay after school. When she didn't come, he went outside to look for her. That's when he had seen the taller boy, the clean-cut muscular one. The older boy had called to him from his truck. Brent made his way over to ask what he wanted. As Brent approached the cab, several boys jumped out and grabbed him, shoving him into the back of the truck.

"Where do you go to school?" Smokey asked. He had never seen him at his school.

Brent told them that he went to a private school in Virginia, and he was sent there by his father, who was an executive at the coal mine in Keystone. They lived in Bramwell in one of the big mansions built in the late 1800s.

Most of the money from the coalfields never saw the light of day in West Virginia. Wealthy outsiders came to mine the coal, stripped the wealth from the land, and then left.

Smokey and Do What both knew what he meant when he said he lived in Bramwell. Most of the mansions were no longer occupied; most of the wealthy millionaires that had made their fortunes during the coal boom in the late 1800s and early 1900s returned to big cities like New York, Philadelphia, and Boston. But a few families remained to keep drudging coal from the once pristine mountains. The mountains had been leveled and plundered for that beautiful black gold that made a few rich at the expense of the rest. Those who worked the mines remained in the coal camps and surrounding towns like Northfork, Keystone, and Welch. Oil had replaced much of the demand for coal. Even if coal would have still been king, the use of big machines meant that there were fewer jobs for manual labor. Some mining jobs remained, but were in steady decline, especially after World War II had ended some fifteen years earlier.

The current was pulling the canoe along, but the boys hadn't given up paddling. They didn't want to take a chance that the other boys found some other boat stowed away at the cabin. If they could get enough distance between them, they would be far enough away not to be caught even if the boys got back on the river.

The night sky was still lit by the canopy of stars. Without the moonlight, they had to pick their way carefully through the dark.

Brent continued talking. He told them that he was only twelve years old and in the seventh grade. He didn't have any siblings and had never been on the Greenbrier River or in a canoe. He told them that the boys had gagged him and tied him up. He had no idea who the boys were or why they were targeting him. He had never seen them or heard of them before.

Smokey was already trying to figure out what they might be doing taking a young boy from a school. Since they didn't know Brent, it seemed unlikely it had been done as a prank or a joke. The way they tied up Smokey when he came to rescue Brent told him that this was something more serious. But who would want to take him and why? What were they going to do with him anyway?

The night sky was still dark except for the stars, but they needed to make up some time going down the river so that the boys couldn't catch up to them. They paddled hard for twenty minutes but eventually took a break. Do What and Smokey wished that they had another paddle so that Brent could help. With the added weight in the canoe, it was harder to pull all three of them down the river.

Brent offered to help to give them a rest, so Do What handed Brent his paddle to help Smokey. Brent stared at the paddle before putting it in the water. He tried to keep the rhythm with Smokey but kept hitting his paddle. He seemed awkward and uncomfortable with paddling. Smokey gave him some tips on how to hold the paddle and how to pull with each stroke rather than just chop at the water. Smokey was still wet from earlier and didn't want to get more wet from Brent's splashing.

After about ten minutes, Brent pulled the paddle in, tired and frustrated that he was having trouble keeping up with the strokes that Smokey was calling for.

The river was getting rougher. They entered the part of the river where the rapids were larger and the water moved faster. Normally Smokey and Do What would carry the canoe on the river's edge so that they would avoid denting and dinging the aluminum shell. In the dark, navigating the large boulders and rocks was a challenge. But they didn't want to risk stopping, so they continued to paddle. They had already made good time and were close to the spot where Do What's brother would pick them up in the morning.

Do What and Smokey had navigated the rapids once before, but that had been during the daylight at a time of the year when the river was much higher and moving faster, and there were fewer rocks exposed. One of the biggest rapids—they had nicknamed it Killer—was coming up soon, and they both knew it. They hadn't wanted to think about it because one wrong turn and the entire canoe could capsize, or worse, be bent and torn to shreds on the rocks, hurling them down the rapids.

A few years ago, a group of boys thought that they could navigate Killer with large tractor inner tubes. They had a few beers with them on their way down the river. When the rough rapids came, they were not ready for how violent it would be. Two of the six boys drowned. Smokey had known one of them, and he was a great swimmer. Even he couldn't escape the raging rapids. Smokey had thought that perhaps with the water being a little lower, it might make the river less violent but instead it just made it harder to navigate. Many of the exposed jagged rocks were like teeth protruding up out of the churning water.

Smokey turned to Brent and said, "I hope you're a good swimmer!"

Brent didn't respond and turned to look at Smokey, who was bent backward and using his paddle like a rudder to navigate around the already fierce rapids.

"I don't know how to swim," he said.

Do What turned back and caught a glance of Smokey's eyes. He could tell by the strain in Smokey's face that they were unlikely to get out of this ride without falling in.

"I guess we better not fall out then," Do What shouted, trying to reassure them.

Smokey was nervous. If his friend who was a strong swimmer had drowned, there might be no hope for a non-swimmer to make it through the rapids if the canoe capsized. There was no other option, they had to ride it out.

They were still a few rapids away from Killer, and the waves tossed their canoe to and fro like a balloon on a windy day. No matter how hard they paddled, they were fighting against the powerful current and the hidden rocks just below the surface.

They rounded the first big bend in the river, and the large sudden dip that signaled that Killer was just a few minutes away. Smokey knew they needed as much maneuverability as possible and shouted to Do What to throw out the wet blankets and clothes that were in the plastic bag. Being so soaked in water, it was like there were two other people in the boat. It was almost impossible for Smokey to steer the boat fast enough to avoid colliding with the hidden rocks just below the surface.

The night sky was beginning to brighten. It was the last moment just before dawn where you can sense and see the morning sky getting ready to release itself and call it day. Do What heaved the waterlogged plastic bag over the side of the canoe. It hit with a splash and the current picked it up. It raced ahead of them. For a while, the bag worked as a guide to avoid the rocks ahead. As more water seeped in, it sank beneath the bow and out of sight. The lost weight gave them more control, and Smokey was able to turn the boat in and out of the way of the huge waves.

At the stern, Smokey had to lean back on the rear of the boat to get the paddle in deep enough water to steer the canoe. At times he almost lost his balance and nearly fell in. Smokey had never navigated this part of the river, and each turn revealed another treacherous trap to escape.

Brent crouched on the floor of the center of the canoe. He held the sides of the gunwales of the canoe with such a tight grip that blood appeared on his fingers. He was as white as a ghost and emitted a low cry like a rabbit caught in a hunter's snare.

Do What did his best to pull against the water in the bow of the boat. He was strong and had canoed some white water on the New River. He was drenched. When he glanced back to check on Smokey and Brent, he noticed that the canoe was filling up with water.

"Brent, grab the bailer and scoop out as much water as you can, or we're going to sink!" Do What shouted.

Brent stared in uncertainty, and Smokey tossed the small coffee can they used to bail out the water from the canoe. Brent seemed confused, but started to scoop water out and throw it overboard. The water was entering the boat at three times the rate he was scooping it out.

"Bail the water faster, Brent!" Smokey shouted.

Brent scooped as fast as his small violin-playing hands could go. Once he started to get the rhythm, he was actually getting ahead of the water that was coming into the canoe.

The canoe rose and fell on the rapids. At times, they couldn't see anything before them besides a wall of water. They had made it this far, and they were determined not to give up now, but the Killer rapid was still ahead of them, churning with fury. Even if they wanted to get to the side of the river, the strong current would make it impossible. They would have to take their chances and ride the wild ride if they were going to get through this part of the river.

Smokey's hands were aching, and he could feel blisters forming under his palm from gripping the paddle so tightly. The pain seared him, but he paddled on. Sun rays lit the morning sky. A soft hue of blue light began to fill the river, which helped them navigate around rocks. Unfortunately, the worst was still to come.

With each rise and fall of the rapids, they came closer to Killer, the very spot where those two boys never made it out alive just a couple years earlier. Smokey tried to keep the image out of his head, but he saw Jimmy's face in his mind and had a hard time shaking the image of the strong boy and his friend who had been no match for these turbulent waters.

There was a small lull in the rapids, which gave them a sense of relief, perhaps even a small sense of hope. Smokey knew that it was about to get worse, this was the calm before the storm. The little canoe meant to guide them gently down the river to catch some fish and relax was no match for these intense waves. Canoes are easy to tip over on still water and nearly impossible to keep afloat with even a little rocking and swaying.

Smokey took a deep breath and braced himself for Killer. Jimmy's confident demeanor entered his mind, and Smokey wondered if he had felt the same sense of smallness that Smokey now felt headed to this part of the river. Maybe his cockiness had prevented him from understanding what he was about to enter.

The rapids were coming again, and the water rushed in faster than Brent could keep up with. He continued scooping and tossing the water back over the edge of the canoe. Smokey wondered if Do What was thinking about Jimmy or the water ride ahead or if he was lost in his thoughts as he often was. Maybe it was better that way. He didn't want either of them to lose their focus, not now.

The first large series of rapids tossed the small craft back and forth like a paper boat, indifferent to the boys contained within. They managed to miss the first set of rocks near the head of the rapids, but the huge dip almost bent the canoe in half. The hull of the boat hit the bottom of the rapids with a thud that nearly sent Brent out of the canoe. He shrieked and grabbed the canoe's side; the coffee can sailed through the air and into the water. He held tightly to the side.

Smokey used what remaining strength he had to steer the small canoe away from the rocks. The rapids were unavoidable, but he knew if they hit the rock ahead, they would all be tossed into the water. With each wave that came, an even larger one seemed to follow. They left one wave after another until the waves and rapids seemed to blend together, and Smokey could no longer tell which were rocks and which were just swells.

The canoe scraped along a rock, causing an intense sound like the moan of a woman dying. He paddled harder to avoid it, but his strength was failing. He hoped that the small vessel could hold up just a little longer. In the distance, he saw the rapids they called Killer. It was five times bigger than any they had already passed, and he felt a deep sense of doubt that he had to battle away when he saw it. No, he told himself. No, he wasn't going to give up. No, he wasn't gonna overthink it. No, he wasn't gonna let them die here, just no.

He pushed the image of Jimmy out of his mind and thought of his parents, his siblings, and how much he wanted to see the world and everything in it. He wasn't ready to go.

He gripped as tight as he could and paddled faster than he had ever done before. He had a huge surge of strength that he thought he had lost. His canoe lunged forward and missed the first huge rock, making it through the narrow passage of safety between two boulders. He wanted to shout in victory but knew that it wasn't time to celebrate yet. While the near miss had been miraculous, two more huge rapids were coming up just ahead.

The water dropped and sent them down a huge waterfall-type of drop that felt like a vertical freefall. Smokey nearly slid out of his seat and down towards the center of the canoe. He was able to brace himself with his feet, but Brent slid forward and nearly knocked Do What over the bow. Smokey shouted to hang on, but the roar of the rapids drowned out his feeble yell.

They were headed for a huge boulder that if they hit directly would bend their aluminum boat in half and send them sailing into the water. Do What used the paddle to brace from the impact, but the sudden force snapped the wooden paddle in half like a popsicle stick. The jolt pivoted the boat away from the rock, which spared them the fatal blow. Smokey was on his own now to steer the canoe through the final rapid, the killer that took Jimmy.

He tried not to picture Jimmy's face while he paddled. He thought about the huge fish that got away. He thought about how he was supposed to be famous. His fame was supposed to come from victory, not in the newspaper as some tragedy. He wanted to live and that thought propelled him.

The huge set of rapids tossed them back and forth, and they hit almost every rock, pounding and scraping the small canoe. He thought for a moment what Do What's brother might say when he saw the canoe all banged up and dented. He laughed a little because if he did see the canoe, that would mean they had made it.

They hit the largest rapid, and it tossed the canoe into the air and spun them around backward. Smokey couldn't steer anymore, and they were at the mercy of the rapids.

The boat was tossed into the air, and all three of them were ejected from the canoe. A large wave sent them sailing ahead of the boat.

Smokey felt his feet hit the rocks below and he struggled for air. He swam for the surface and gasped as he pushed against the rocks with his feet.

He remembered that if you fall out of a boat, you should point your feet down the river in order to protect your head. Maybe he had heard this from his brother who seemed to know a little about a lot. He was usually skeptical of his brother's advice, but at this moment he trusted him.

His feet hit the rocks immediately. He searched for Do What and caught sight of him three boat lengths down the river. He searched for Brent but saw nothing but the small coffee can they had lost before. He twisted and turned, but the rapids made it impossible to see beyond a few feet. He wondered if he had done the right thing to rescue Brent from the boys only to drown him in the river. He didn't have much time to think, though, because he was still a prisoner of the rapids.

It felt like an eternity though it was merely moments later when Killer spat him out. Just ahead of him, Smokey saw Do What trying to pull himself out of the water onto the rocky shore. There was no sign of Brent.

Smokey twisted and turned, searching for the boy. He saw a small tennis shoe in the water. The rapids must have knocked him out of his shoes. Smokey swam back towards the rapids calling Brent's name, but he was no match for the current.

"Brent!" he shouted.

"Over there!" Do What shouted back.

Brent's still body floated facedown out of the rapids towards Smokey. He dove under to pull him out. He wrapped his arms around his chest and under his arm to pull his limp body to the rocky shore where Do What stood.

Once he had dragged Brent onto the riverbank, he turned him onto his back.

"Is he breathing?" Do What shouted.

He wasn't. Brent was limp and seemed even more frail lying there. Smokey had only heard of CPR but had no idea if it really worked.

"Come on, Brent, breathe!" he said.

He knelt over his body, shaking him, but there was no response. He instinctively pulled back Brent's head and blew into his mouth. "Breathe," he said. With each breath, Brent's chest rose but his eyes remained closed and his body lay still. Smokey blew another breath to fill Brent's lungs; still nothing. His heart was racing and beating in his chest. "Breathe, Brent, breathe."

Brent's chest rose and fell as Smokey forced the air back into his body. Do What stood over him taking in deep breaths as if to aid him.

"Come on, Brent," Do What whispered. "You can do it."

Smokey took one last deep breath and blew. There was still no life in his body.

"Pinch his nose," Do What said. Do What had read about CPR in one of the special *National Geographic* magazines about the Coast Guard. Their specialized training saved someone's life on a mission at sea.

Smokey pinched Brent's nose and gave one more breath. Smokey knelt over him and waited. He held his own breath, imagining he could pass it to Brent laying on the ground. There was no movement, and both Do What and Smokey held still for what seemed like minutes.

Brent suddenly convulsed, and water shot out of his mouth all over Smokey's face. He coughed out what seemed like a canoe full of water. He heaved and sputtered, then vomited. But he was breathing.

Do What turned to Smokey and sighed a deep sound of relief. Brent tried to sit up quickly, not certain where he was. It was as if he was still on the canoe in the middle of the rapids.

"You're okay," Smokey reassured him. Brent breathed heavily, in and out, a wild and disoriented look in his eyes.

"Did we make it?" Brent asked.

Both Do What and Smokey laughed and said, "Yeah we made it."

At that moment, the canoe popped up out of the rapids and beached itself right on the rocky shore next to them. It was still in decent shape but the scrapes along the bottom showed where it had dragged against the rocks. It was incredible that it wasn't twisted and sunk to the bottom of the river. It was a miracle that they survived.

They all laughed when the canoe washed ashore, giddy to have escaped for the second time that day.

CHAPTER 6

As they caught their breath, a few of their belongings washed up on the shore. They gathered what they could and carried the canoe to a level spot. They found a fragment of a broken paddle, part of the one that Do What broke against the rock. The other paddle was nowhere to be seen.

Brent sat on a rock in the sun, trying to warm his body while Do What and Smokey turned the canoe over to empty it of all the water and walked it up to a sandy spot on the river.

Away from Brent, they spoke in hushed voices to talk about what to do next. They weren't sure how they would get the canoe further down the river without a paddle. They thought they might be able to carry the canoe part of the way, but the sides of the riverbank were slick, and there was no way to get up to the road from here. Suddenly, they heard a shout from Brent.

"The paddle!" he shouted, pointing to the river.

Do What didn't hesitate. He jumped to his feet and bolted down to the water, diving in like an Olympic swimmer. The paddle was being carried downstream along the far side of the river.

Brent rose to his feet and cheered Do What on.

Do What reached the paddle and held it over his head in victory. It was some kind of luck they were having, and Smokey wished they had a poker game to join. If things stayed this way, they would be sure to win the whole pot.

No sooner had Smokey thought that and Do What arrived at the shore when he saw a the truck at the top of the road by the side of the bank. Four boys peered down at them.

"There they are!" Hans shouted.

The spot on the road was the last bend before the road diverged from the path of the river. Do What and Smokey rushed to grab the canoe and launch it into the water. Brent hesitated at the water's edge. Smokey grabbed him gently by the arm and helped him in as fast as he could.

"Get in! It's gonna be alright," Smokey said.

In a matter of seconds, the three boys were back in the water. Hans and two of his younger brothers were making their way down the hill toward the shore, but it was steep and the rocks made it difficult to move fast.

"Stop them!" Hans shouted.

Smokey paddled hard. Both Do What and Brent cheered him on. The river bent up ahead, and if they kept going, they would be out of sight in a matter of no time. Without a boat, Frank and his brothers in the truck couldn't catch them. In a few more moments, the canoe disappeared.

Once they cleared the bend in the river, Do What turned to Brent and asked, "What did you do to them to piss them off?"

Brent shrugged and said nothing. Smokey had been trying to make the connection to the eldest brother, Frank, since he first saw him in the cabin. He looked familiar, but Smokey still couldn't make out how he knew him. He was too old to be someone he knew from school, and he didn't seem like he stayed in Keystone or Northfork. Maybe he had kin there.

It was driving him crazy not knowing who he was. Smokey tried to remember which family had four sons down in the county, but he didn't remember ones with brothers his age and older. He scanned his mind through all the places he knew of in the vicinity of McDowell County. The county included many of the coal mining communities of southern West Virginia with countless hollows tucked in between the rugged Appalachian Mountains. Smokey vaguely remembered one set of brothers that disappeared back when he was in elementary school, but it had been so long ago. He was drawing a blank and couldn't remember their names or how he knew of them. No matter how

much Smokey racked his brain and insisted on finding a clue, he came up with nothing but questions.

They were making good time and hoped they
would make the rendezvous at their meetup spot
with Do What's brother before the brothers caught
up to them. They were scheduled to be picked up by
Mike near the town of Hinton just a bit farther down
the river from that spot. But knowing Mike, if they
were not there at the time he was, he would leave
them and they would be stuck at the hands of Hans
and his brothers.

With only one paddle, Smokey was the only one
who could move the boat forward. Do What and
Brent chatted about trivial things, mainly the geography that Do What studied in his *National Geographic*
magazines. Brent seemed to know a great deal about
the world, and Do What seemed to appreciate his
interest in maps, travel, and the various countries
around the globe. Smokey smiled because Do What
didn't seem to find many people his age that appre-
ciated his sense of wonder. Though Brent was a few
years younger, he seemed to appreciate his interests.

Smokey paddled nonstop and continued puz-
zling over Hans and his brothers. He was sweating
with the sun just over the top of them. His stomach
started to churn with hunger. He hadn't had any food
since the fish they caught the day before. He longed
for a couple of his mother's biscuits and gravy and a
nice hot cup of coffee.

He loved the savory flavor of his mother's gravy. She had what she called a secret ingredient, which made it taste so good. When he was little, on the weekends, Smokey would sit on the counter and watch her cook and chat with her about the day and she would make breakfast for the family. Every time he asked her to tell him the secret, she would always say the secret ingredient was love. One morning, he spotted her pouring coffee into the gravy. He never mentioned it to anyone and didn't let on that he knew what the ingredient was. He was content with her explanation: it was just love.

He had always felt grateful that he had such a wonderful family, though now they were all starting to grow more distant with each person having their own lives. His brother and sister were seldom home now that they were married, and his other brother was preparing for the army. He himself was home less and less now that he was in high school. He felt a bit guilty for wanting to leave home and go see the world, but his wanderlust grew stronger every day, and he had big hopes of traveling the world. His stomach called to him, and he thought what he wouldn't do for those biscuits and gravy right then.

They were about two miles out from the spot where Mike had agreed to meet them. He would be furious about the damage to the canoe, and Smokey figured he would have to use some of the savings from his paper route to buy a new paddle and repair any damage to the boat.

As Smokey paddled, his hunger turned to anger when he thought about the boys taking Brent from his school and tying him up. He used the anger to paddle even faster. They would have to convince Mike to drive Brent home, which they knew would be virtually impossible without a bribe. His savings would have to be used again to give him gas money and probably buy him lunch. With each stroke, he grew more and more mad.

Smokey had been so focused on his hunger he had forgotten that Do What and Brent were in the boat. He barely heard them calling his name when they pointed out that the boat was beginning to fill with water. The boat had looked relatively unscathed by the rapids, but a small leak in the seam of the boat was allowing the water to seep in. Without the coffee can, bailing the water out would be a challenge.

Both Do What and Brent cupped their hands to scoop the water out and over the edge. Smokey paddled even faster. Despite the boys' constant scooping, the water was rapidly filling the canoe. There was almost two inches of water in the boat. They had almost a mile to go before they would reach the meeting spot. With the extra weight of the water, Smokey had a hard time keeping the pace he had set.

Smokey recognized where they were, and he could see the clearing up ahead where they were supposed to beach the canoe and be picked up by Mike. The parking spot was visible by now, but there was no sign of the truck. The water was now up to their ankles. They were only one hundred yards away from shore, so close they could almost throw a rock to it. With each paddle, the boat sunk just a little bit more. Smokey closed his eyes for a second and hoped that when he opened them Mike's truck would be there.

"Come on," he said under his breath. "You can make it."

They were nearly there. Just then, a truck pulled up, sending the dirt and gravel flying. Smokey froze. Instead of Mike, he saw Hans and his brothers jumping out of their truck.

The boys were now almost completely submerged, and Smokey's arms were burning from paddling. The other boys were so focused scooping water, they hadn't noticed the truck pull up. When the canoe hit the shore, they raised their hands up over their head and cheered in victory, not knowing what was now in store for them.

Suddenly, Hans and his brothers grabbed the canoe so the boys couldn't get away. They pulled it up on to the shore.

"Thought you could get away?" Hans said. He had a gloating smile, sure that the victory was his. He grabbed Brent by the arm and dragged him from the canoe.

Do What scurried to help Brent, but the twins grabbed him and pulled his hands behind his back.

Smokey sat in the canoe filled with water and didn't move. He stared at Frank. He recognized the scowl on his face but still couldn't place it.

Brent pulled his arm free from Hans. Hans looked at him with a surprised look and dared him to try something.

Brent had survived the rapids, drowned, and been brought back to life; he wasn't as afraid as he had once been. He looked like he'd grown an inch since the night before.

Hans was not amused. He grabbed Brent, put his hands behind his back, and led him to his older brother, who was like a general on a battlefield waiting for the prisoners to be paraded before him.

"This little game is over," Frank said. "Put the little punk in the truck." Hans began to lead Brent to the truck when Smokey stood from the water-filled canoe.

"Let him go," Smokey said in a low but confident voice.

Frank cocked his head and twitched his eye, saying without words, "Who do you think you are?"

Frank stared at the water-logged vessel that had somehow survived the most impossible rapids. Smokey walked up the center of the canoe and stepped confidently onto the shore. He was also standing a little taller than the night before.

"You boys had your fun, and this will just be another little fish that got away," Frank said. His muscles rippled under his tight, white T-shirt. Smokey's arms seemed to hang like toothpicks in comparison, but he didn't flinch.

"This is what is going to happen: you're going to let Brent go, and you're gonna get back in that sorry excuse for a truck and leave and not come back," Smokey said.

Frank clenched his teeth and took a step forward. Do What and Brent, struggling and dragging their feet so that they couldn't be moved easily, were still being held by the other brothers. Frank reached into his back pocket and with one flick opened the blade of a large pocketknife and held it to Smokey's face.

"You are all mouthy, boy," he said.

He stepped forward and grabbed Smokey's wrist. Do What and Brent protested and tried to get loose from their captors. Frank held the knife towards Smokey's throat. Smokey was tired and wet but held himself defiant and still. He tried not to show any fear, but a slight tremble in the corner of his lip escaped anyway.

A loud obnoxious horn blared from the road just above them. A rusted old Chevy sped around the corner and slid into the gravel just behind the other truck. It came to a stop, and the dust rose and covered the boys.

Mike jumped out of the truck with a rifle in one hand and a beer can in the other. He fired a warning shot.

They all froze, and Smokey pulled himself free. Do What and Brent pushed the other boys away, who were now cowering from the ringing of the shot.

With a cigarette hanging from his lips, Mike said. "Sorry I'm late to the party, boys, but I had to stop to take a piss."

"Put the weapon down," Hans called.

Do What's brother didn't like to be told what to do, so of course he aimed the gun in the direction of Hans.

"Do you like to dance?" Mike asked. He aimed at Hans's feet and fired. All the brothers leaped and danced away as the gravel flung in their direction.

"It's always good to dance at a party," he said, laughing like a lunatic. He seemed to be enjoying this.

Smokey darted away from Frank and hurried over to the Chevy. Hans and the other brothers hid behind their truck, calling for their older brother to come.

Frank folded the pocketknife and walked slowly back to his truck. He had accepted that this battle was lost, but his slow saunter said he was far from giving up the war. He would be even more dangerous now that he had been defeated for a second time.

Do What and Brent cheered and flipped off the truck as it sped down the road. Smokey walked up to Do What, Brent, and Mike, who were all reeling from their victory. He knew, however, that their celebration was somewhat premature. He knew Hans and his brothers would be back out looking for Brent as soon as they had regrouped. Next time they might be armed. Smokey was relieved to see Mike, but he also knew now that Mike was involved, it was going to complicate things.

Smokey wondered if they should just head to the school to return Brent, but then he looked over at Mike, who was essentially a functional drunk with a loaded gun and a boy that was kidnapped from his hometown. If the law was looking for this kid, Mike, Do What, and Smokey might look guilty. He worried the police might shoot first before they asked any questions.

"You boys owe me a canoe and paddles," Mike said, flicking the ashes off his cigarette.

He turned and headed for the truck.

Do What and Brent walked down to the river to empty the canoe and carry it up to the truck. It was damaged, but they figured they could get Smokey's dad to help them patch it up.

Mike guzzled what was left of the beer and flung the empty can to the side of the road. He opened up the driver's side door, threw the rifle behind the bench seat, and hurried the boys to get in. It was obvious that Mike had been out all night and had not been to bed yet. He seemed to be a bit more sleepy than drunk, which seemed nearly impossible since the alcohol was seeping from his pores and he could barely stand steady without swaying.

Mike tossed the keys to Smokey and said, "Here, you drive. I'm gonna take a nap." He stumbled to the passenger side and told Brent and Do What to scoot over.

Smokey had driven his father's truck many times and often drove him to Bluefield even though he didn't have a driver's license. For the longest time, Smokey just thought his dad wanted Smokey to drive him so he would learn how to drive the double-clutch properly. His oldest brother had taught him when he was just twelve years old, and he had to push the gas pedal and clutch with his toes while he sat on a stack of books. Later, Smokey found out that his dad didn't know how to drive and figured when Smokey's older brother left, he needed another young driver to get him to and from places.

Smokey started the truck and put it into first gear, and the truck lunged to a start. Before they even left the gravel, Mike was passed out.

Smokey headed back toward Northfork, not sure where to go next. If they headed to Virginia to take Brent to the boarding school, they might be accused of being the ones who had taken him, or worse they might catch up to Hans and his brothers. Smokey headed towards home. They drove with the windows down. It was cold with the wind whipping through the cabin of the truck, but that was preferable to the musty smell of liquor that oozed from Mike's body.

They drove for a while in silence, listening to Mike's drunken snore that hissed and huffed from the passenger's side.

The road was curvy, and the boys shifted from side to side as Smokey drove. Mike somehow slept through it all. It was nearly twenty minutes before they broke the silence of the quiet cabin.

"What are we going to do Smoke?" Do What asked, then he turned to Brent. "I bet your parents are really worried."

Brent had been just as quiet as the rest of them. It took him a moment to answer.

"I don't even think they know I'm missing."

Smokey and Do What exchanged shocked glances. Brent was only twelve. Certainly his parents must have been worried sick even after just a few hours, not to mention to have him missing overnight. Smokey wondered how it would be possible for it to go unnoticed if Brent was missing.

Brent went on to explain that he was waiting for his nanny to pick him up from school and take him to his violin practice. He hated violin, but it was a good excuse not to go home. His parents were often so busy with their own lives that they didn't see him for days at a time. His father's work kept him traveling a great deal, and his mother was often doing charitable work or shopping or traveling away from home. He was an only child and was seldom even talked to when they were at home. Brent told them that he lived in Bramwell but didn't really have any friends there. Most of the time he was away at boarding school and didn't see his parents. He guessed that when he wasn't there to be picked up, his nanny just assumed he went with a friend or had their driver pick him up for his lesson.

Smokey couldn't imagine being forgotten by his parents, but he did know how it felt to be invisible. He was the baby of the family and received almost all of the attention when he was born. He was a Christmas surprise, born almost seven years after his other siblings. They weren't planning for another child; in fact, his mother had been told she couldn't have any more children after his older brother was born. After his ornery older brother, Smokey's mother had been delighted to welcome Smokey, a happier, more content baby, into the family. His mother called him her little miracle and treated him like the gift that she thought he was.

His brothers and sisters, however, weren't always as adoring as she was. They didn't like how much he was babied when he was young and how he often got away with more at his age than they did. Because he was adored by most of the women in his family, his brother picked on him a great deal. But even his teasing was balanced by what felt like his duty to pro-tect his younger brother. He was grateful that it was Mike and not his own brother that had rescued them from Hans and his brothers. If Smokey's brother had been there, he would have lectured him about how stupid he was for getting into trouble again and how he had to save his tail one more time.

Smokey was never trying to get mixed up in trou-ble, but it was like flies on a hog—always present. He was grateful that his brother had shown him how to drive and that he was pretty good at it.

They drove the winding roads back to Northfork. He was grateful it was Sunday morning and most folks were still in church, leaving the roads empty. You'd never catch Smokey dead in a church. He fig-ured if he stepped inside, he might just burn up in flames right then and there.

Smokey hadn't forgotten Do What's question about what they would do about Brent but was still formulating a plan before he spoke. Do What was used to Smokey taking his time responding, and it didn't much bother him, but it drove everyone else crazy. His father would often ask if the boy needed a hearing cone like the old folks used. He heard them speak but he was often just in another world, plan-ning out each scenario before he responded.

"The last place they would look for Brent is in Cinder Bottom, so we should head there," Smokey said. He figured they would need a plan to return him to his house so that his parents wouldn't even know he was missing. According to Brent, they were out of town but would be back that night for Sunday dinner, which was the one meal they had together. Even if they got Brent home again safe, Smokey felt they needed to be certain that Hans and his brothers wouldn't get to him again.

Smokey wondered once again why Hans would be after Brent in the first place. He was about to ask Brent what his father did so that he could put the pieces together when a police car showed up in his review mirror. He watched carefully to see if it was Sheriff Donnie from Cinder Bottom. The sheriff often drove this road since his mama lived down that way and he would visit her on Sundays. She was so proud of him because he was a law man, but she didn't really understand that he was the sheriff for Cinder Bottom, the most notorious red-light district this side of the Mississippi. He wanted to stay in her good graces, so he never missed a Sunday with her.

But when the car approached the truck, Smokey made out that it was a police car from Virginia, a state trooper.

"Awe, damn," Smokey said. "We got a trooper on our tail."

They turned and looked back.

"Oh hell! What are we gonna do?" Do What said.

"Reach into the glove box and hand me a cigarette," Smokey said. Do What handed him a pack of

Pall Malls, and Smokey grabbed the lighter that was just above the ash tray. He lit up and began to puff. Brent coughed and sputtered.

"That smells terrible," Brent gasped.

"That's the point," he said. "We gotta hide the alcohol smell."

Smokey knew that they might get away with driving without a license, but if they suspected they were drinking too, they would probably take them in. He told them to act natural, or at least as natural as two teenagers and a missing boy could act. Virginia State troopers were notorious for being tough, but he was out of his jurisdiction here in West Virginia. If they were lucky, he would just pass them by and that would be that. They had the canoe in the back, and they would tell him the truth if he pulled them over: they were just floating the river trying to catch a few smallmouth bass and were headed home.

Smokey told them to remain calm, but on the inside, he knew that more than likely Hans and his brothers had tipped off the trooper and told the police that Smokey had kidnapped Brent. They would go to jail for sure.

Smokey remained calm and took a long drag on his cigarette, hoping the police car would just pass him by. The closer the car got, the more anxious he became. Though he was tall for a fifteen-year-old, if you looked at Smokey, he had a baby face, and it almost always caused suspicion.

Brent was fidgety and was bouncing his leg up and down. Do What placed his hand on his knee to calm him down so that he wouldn't draw attention if they were pulled over. Brent must not have noticed because he looked at Do What and quickly apologized.

The police car was closer now, and Smokey remained calm, taking long drags off his cigarette, even holding his arm out the window to flick the ashes as he had seen his uncle Sammy do.

Be calm, Smokey, he said to himself silently. Smokey was more worried that he might get caught driving without a license and lose his chance to get one than he was if they were looking for Brent. If he didn't get his license when he was sixteen, that might mean he would be stuck more often in Northfork, and he wanted to get out more than anything he could imagine.

If they got caught, he would ask Brent to tell the truth, though it did sound a bit far-fetched. Besides the canoe in the back, they had no evidence of their encounter with Hans and his brothers at the cabin. Nor did they have evidence that they had caught the largest smallmouth bass in the Greenbrier River or that they had survived the killer rapids and brought Brent back to life. All of it seemed out of this world, and he knew that it might be better for them all if the trooper just kept going.

The police car came closer, and Smokey let his foot off his gas slightly to signal to the trooper to pass. His father had taught him that those who want to pass will. He saw the sunglasses of the trooper in his rear-view mirror now, and he wondered if this would be it. Mike snored and snorted, oblivious. Smokey wondered how much of the morning's events he would even remember.

The trooper sped up now and pulled up alongside Smokey. He didn't make eye contact and just kept driving. Smokey took a long drag on his cigarette as if to say, "This is all normal." The trooper pulled alongside the truck on a long straight away, glanced at Smokey, gave a Southern nod, and then sped past them. Smokey hissed a sigh of relief and Brent and Do What whooped in victory. Mike contributed a loud snore.

Smokey knew that they had to get Mike's truck back, but they also needed to figure out what to do with Brent. Both Brent and Do What were now drifting off to sleep along with Mike. They had a ways to go but he figured with the night they had they both needed the sleep.

Smokey was trying to figure out what Hans and his brothers' next move would be. If this was more than just a prank, which he was certain was the case now, they would be coming for Brent. He had wondered if they were out to get some sort of ransom, since Brent mentioned his father was traveling all the time and they lived in one of those big mansions in Bramwell. They had probably been eyeing him for some time, waiting for the opportune time to kidnap him and hold him for ransom. If that was the case, why did they bring him down to the Greenbrier River, to a small out-of-the way cabin? There had to be a reason they were there. If they had already initiated the ransom request, they must have had a place and time to deliver Brent, but where and when?

These thoughts rushed in and out of Smokey's mind at such an astonishing rate he didn't have a moment to think about being tired. He was processing so many scenarios that he wasn't sure which one to follow.

The road to Cinder Bottom was calm, being Sunday and all. He really enjoyed the way the mountain pass meandered and danced around the river, He admired the gorges and how the trees dotted the winding road. He recalled the numerous trips that he and his pa made to fish smallmouth bass from the river. He felt a pang of disappointment when he thought of the monstrous fish they had retrieved from the river. Though his body was cold from being in the water, his blood still boiled hot at the thought of Hans and his brothers stealing his prized catch. He wouldn't forget, and he was determined to figure out what they were up to.

The thought of revenge grew as he drove, and he ached to find out where they were headed now. He had wondered if they might have gone to fetch a rifle and if they were returning now to search for them. He figured they had a plan already brewing, and he had to get ahead of their thinking. He wanted to wake Do What to ask him if he had some thoughts, but his gentle snore made him decide to leave him to rest.

Smokey was driving faster and faster as his brain raced to solve the mystery of Hans and his brothers. He was taking the curves a little faster than before, and the boys slid back and forth on the bench seat of the truck, all still fast asleep. The trees flew by as he took every curve like a race car driver in his final lap in a race. The tires screeched with each turn.

As he rounded the next curve, a large eight-point buck with a rack big enough to hang the coats and hats of an entire family leapt in front of the truck. He swerved to avoid hitting the giant whitetail deer. The truck went off the highway down the slope toward the lower road. The truck careened out of control, and he managed to avoid crashing directly into a large black walnut tree as he sped down the side of the embankment.

The truck nearly rolled as it skidded back and forth, finally coming to a stop at the bottom of a small road that wound along the creek. The narrow strip of washed-out pavement once served as the main road before the two-lane highway was built. The entire truck was rocking, and the boys jolted from their sleep to a state of terror. Mike just yawned when the truck came to a stop.

The truck came to rest on the lower road, and Smokey was white as a ghost. They had miraculously landed without a scratch except for the canoe, which was tossed from the bed of the truck into an overgrown thicket along the bank of the creek.

Mike stretched and looked around. "Why did you take the low road, Smokey? It's a lot faster on the high road."

Smokey didn't respond. He just turned to him, stunned, and then laughed. He was grateful to have escaped death, yet again.

Do What turned to him and said, "What happened?" Brent was also as white as a ghost.

The color slowly returned to Smokey when he realized they were safe and that there was no damage to the truck or the passengers.

Smokey opened the door and motioned for Do What and Brent to help him retrieve the canoe and load it back into the bed of the truck. It was wedged in between two small saplings, which prevented it from landing in the water below. They tried to free it, but it was wedged in tightly. Smokey climbed up to the first limb of the tree to try to loosen it from the branches. Luckily the saplings were fairly young and green, and the canoe was easy to rock free from its resting spot.

While perched up on his tree, he saw in the distance a familiar truck: Hans and his brothers were barreling down the road. He signaled for Brent and Do What to duck down. He leapt from the tree just as the pickup sped by with the load of boys in the back. One of the boys steadied himself in the truck bed up against the back of the cab while he gripped a rifle with both his hands. The truck with Smokey and the boys was situated so low down below the main road that from above you couldn't spot it, so Hans and his crew raced past them without detecting a thing.

"What was it, Smokey?" Brent asked.

Do What knew already, that it was the brothers. He grabbed the canoe and motioned for Brent to help.

"It's Hans and his brothers. They're headed for Northfork," Smokey answered. Do What helped him carry the canoe back to the truck.

Mike got out of the passenger's seat. He looked into his packet of Pall Malls and then hit the pack against his palm. When a cigarette popped out, he pulled the narrow cylinder free and slowly guided it to his lips. Mike lit the cigarette, looked at the boys, and said, "Which one of you pansies has been pilfering my cigarettes?"

The boys looked at each other and shrugged. How could he possibly have known one was missing when he probably didn't even remember where he was last night?

Mike climbed in the driver's seat, and they all jumped in the cab and drove down the lower road back to town. The lower road was still intact, though it was covered in weeds and some fallen branches in some spots. Smokey remembered Pa talking about what it was like when the only roads in McDowell County were the lower roads. He thought about the long treks that anyone had to make just to go from one end of the county to the other.

They rejoined the upper road when there was a clear spot and headed back toward Cinder Bottom. Perhaps the brothers figured that they were headed to Bramwell to drop Brent back at his parent's home instead of returning him to his school in Virginia. Once they found out he wasn't there, they would come looking for him all over the county.

Smokey knew that Mike had no interest in what shenanigans they were involved in. He only wanted to get some shuteye before his afternoon at the beer joint began. He would drop them and head down the road to Cinder Bottom to find a card game and a quart of moonshine somewhere. Brent, Do What, and Smokey would be on their own.

Smokey wondered if they should go to Sheriff Donnie and get him involved but he knew that the sheriff would think they were just a couple of boys blowing things out of proportion. Not only would he disregard their ideas, but he would probably say they were just making up the whole story about the fish, the cabin, the brothers, and the rapids. He knew it sounded a bit far-fetched; even he was struggling to believe the trouble they had gotten themselves into. They just wanted to have a nice weekend floating the river, catching a few fish. However, now that they were involved, Smokey was determined to figure out how to help Brent.

When they arrived in Northfork, Mike barely slowed the truck down to let the boys jump out of the cab before he sped down the road towards Cinder Bottom.

Cinder was the kind of place that you could find a good time any time of day. It was only 11:00 a.m., but Mike acted like he had missed a good part of the party and didn't want to waste anymore time with these boys than he had to.

When they all jumped out, he held his hand out the window, waiting for Do What to produce the five dollars he owed him. Do What reached into his secret pocket, which was sewed into the inside of his trousers and where he kept his money, and handed it to him. Mike flipped the bird and drove down the road.

CHAPTER 7

The town of Northfork was just beginning to buzz, and the morning air was brisk. The boys looked like they had been rolled in the dirt wet and smelled from the night and early morning ordeal. They realized that Brent hadn't eaten since he was taken from school on Friday afternoon and that he was probably starving. Before they could figure out a place to get some food, they needed to make sure they were safe. They needed to get off the main street so that they wouldn't be seen if the kidnappers were snooping around looking for them.

They took the path along the railroad tracks to make their way towards Cinder Bottom to avoid being seen by anyone that might know them. If Hans and his brothers started to snoop around and ask questions, the last thing they needed was for people to say that they saw them.

They walked in silence for a bit before Do What started talking about the Andes mountains in Peru, something he had seen in one of his *National Geographic* magazines. He talked about how they survived raids from other tribes and learned to grow potatoes in high elevations. They built intricate stair-like gardens to grow them along the mountain sides. They lived so high in the mountains that it made attacking them difficult.

Do What often talked like he was a walking encyclopedia. He knew more about random stuff than anyone Smokey knew. He would talk for hours if you let him and Smokey would listen so he just kept talking.

Brent seemed to be naturally interested in the conversation and would ask questions about various topics, and Do What was more than happy to oblige. He seemed to relish the fact that Brent wanted to know more. Do What's ability to store information was incredible. He was the smartest person Smokey knew.

Smokey had wondered what Brent's life was like attending an elite private boarding school and living in a big fancy house. He seemed to be a good kid but was unaware of the real world. He didn't seem to mind that Do What talked a lot or that he was overly obsessed with topics that would bore other people his age. Brent seemed to get Do What in a way that Smokey did, like he accepted him for who he was.

Brent did seem a bit frailer than most boys his age, like he hadn't done much in the outdoors. His skin was smooth and pale, except for the dirt from the river. His clothes were finely tailored and his hair trimmed and neat. Smokey wondered what the heck Hans and his brothers wanted from him, but deep down he knew it must be for his money. He wondered if his parents even cared if he was gone or noticed he was missing. From what Brent shared, his parents didn't give a lick about their son and that perhaps him being kidnapped by a bunch of hoodlums would be more of a nuisance than anything else.

When they rounded the last bend along the tracks, they emerged behind Big Ma's place. The parking lot was empty. No one had stirred there this early on a Sunday in a long time. They would have their big Sunday barbecue in the afternoon, so for now it was quiet.

They walked by Ray's store and saw that his truck was gone. He probably hadn't come back from Bluefield yet, where Ray spent every Sunday morning.

They made their way to Geneva's to see about those biscuits and gravy. Smokey knew they couldn't go in the front door as usual since they were so filthy from the night's activities. They headed around to the back door, where the deliveries were made to see if they could catch Jerome, the cook, having a cigarette in the back.

When they arrived, Jerome was sitting on the back steps pulling the last drag from a wilted Pall Mall.

"Hey, Smokey," he said, not noticing they were wet and filthy with dirt. He took his final puff and flicked the butt into a tin can that was filled to the top with discarded cigarettes. Smokey nodded and sat down beside him on the steps.

"Hey, Jerome," Smokey said, acting like they were sitting calmly in a pew at church waiting for the sermon to begin. They both stared off to the woods behind the restaurant and didn't say a word.

"Y'all hungry?" Jerome asked.

Do What nodded his head with excitement.

"Oh, yes, sir," Brent said.

Jerome looked at him sideways and rose to his feet.

"Sir?" Jerome said. "Hell, I like this one. Stay here, I'll be right back." He disappeared back into the kitchen.

Their stomachs growled and the smell of hash browns and bacon cooking made their empty tummy's ache. Smokey could see the desperation that Brent had for food. He had almost forgotten how young he was. He was only twelve and looked even younger. Smokey wondered if he had ever been hungry in his whole life. He had probably eaten the best food while at school and home, and he wondered if he enjoyed country cookin'.

Brent was shaking. He was still wet, and the sun hadn't quite peeked over the trees behind Geneva's. Smokey pointed to a patch of sunshine and told him to stand there and warm up. He was shivering and looked like the hell that they had been through.

Smokey was the youngest of his family, so he never had a little brother. He thought about how much he was teased and picked on by his brothers, but that deep down he felt a sense of protection knowing they were around. He wondered if Brent had ever had that feeling. He felt a sense of responsibility toward him. Maybe the same feeling that Mike had for Do What, even though most of the time he was a jackass toward him. It was that brotherly love that had made Mike stand up for them.

The sun warmed Brent's thin body, and his shivering slowed. In the light, Smokey could detect the underlying sadness that Brent carried with him. It wasn't just about Hans and his brothers; it was something more. He seemed to be holding his breath most of the time and occasionally would exhale just long enough to get some air, but not long enough to relax.

Do What joined Brent in the sun and chatted a bit about the craziness of the night and morning. Smokey could hear them but his mind drifted off to Hans and his brothers and what their next move was. If they did in fact head to Bramwell, once they figured out that Brent wasn't there they would probably hightail it down Route 52 and keep looking.

Jerome busted out the back door with his arms full of food. He had some cups, a pot of coffee, and plates of biscuits and gravy. Do What and Brent sprinted to the rear of the restaurant when they saw him with the vittles. Do What grabbed the door to hold it open, and Smokey helped set the plates of food down on the steps. Before Jerome could pour them all coffee, the boys were tearing into the biscuits and dredging them in the gravy. They ate like stray dogs who had not eaten in weeks. Smokey was fond of biscuits and gravy, a normal meal for him at home, and the black coffee warmed his bones. He hadn't felt so grateful for food in all of his life.

"You boys enjoy. I gotta get back to work," Jerome said before ducking back into the screened door of the kitchen. He stopped and poked his head out again. "Hey, Smokey. Some guys were looking for you a bit earlier this morning."

Smokey almost choked but composed himself quickly. "What'd they want?"

"On't know. I heard 'em yammerin' on about it to Ms. Geneva up front at the counter. They was askin' if she had seen some boys who were wet and dirty. Ms. Geneva told them boys she hadn't seen anyone like that around here." With that, he closed the door and went back to work.

Smokey looked at Do What, and they both knew they had to get Brent to a hiding spot so they could think. Smokey thought that they might take him back to his house. His ma would feed them and give Do What and Brent some dry clothes, but Smokey knew she would also ask a lot of questions, namely about Brent, like where he was from, where his kin were from, and what his father did.

She was like that; she knew just about everything that went on in Northfork and wouldn't stop until she was able to find at least one connection that he had to someone she knew or some family she might have where he was from. She had a way of remembering even the smallest details of family relations. She knew who people married, where they left to when they did leave Northfork, and probably how many kids were in each family. She was like a walking encyclopedia of the who's who in all of McDowell County. Smokey couldn't chance her figuring out who Brent was, at least not before he did.

They devoured all of the food and coffee, which was a first for Brent. He said he was only allowed tea, never coffee, and he spit the first drink out and said it tasted awful and didn't know why anyone would like it. But he finished his cup so he could get warm and wash down the last bites of his biscuits. Smokey took the plates and cups to the kitchen door and signaled for Jerome. He came and retrieved them. Smokey thanked him, and offered to come by and bring Jerome money, but he didn't have any at the moment. Jerome waved him on and said not to worry about it. Smokey inquired about the boys that were looking for him.

"How many boys were looking for us?" Smokey asked.

"Well, there were only two boys, a tall muscular fella and a smaller pint-size version of him, probably brothers, but there was a truckload of others," he said.

"How long ago did they leave?" Smokey asked.

"Ah, maybe an hour or so," Jerome said. Smokey thanked him again and headed back to Brent and Do What. He wondered if the brothers had made it to Bramwell and back that quick. It was a Sunday, and the road would be less busy, but the winding road would take at least twenty-five minutes to get there. Perhaps they had stopped by on their way out, but if that was the case, they would be headed back this way in no time once they discovered Brent wasn't there.

Smokey led Brent and Do What down the back road behind Geneva's toward Big Ma's just on the other side of the street. He wanted to be sure to stay off the main road so that Hans and his brothers didn't spot them. With their bellies full, they made their way down the alley. Smokey figured they would head toward Northfork on the train tracks to avoid being seen, but he didn't know exactly where they were headed. He just wanted to get away and out of sight to give them time to think about their next move.

It was still a little early for the girls at Big Ma's place to be setting up for the weekly family gathering. Smokey and Do What loved being a part of the cookout where there would be barbecue, root beer, and a lot of cards being played. Big Ma had been the madam of the house for decades and treated her girls as family, the type of family that she had once longed for.

The house was still quiet, and Smokey led the boys past her place and made their way towards the train tracks. The train ran once on Sundays usually just after noon, so they had plenty of time to walk the tracks free of worry that it might pass their way. There had been a woman that was walking home from Cinder Bottom to Northfork who was struck by the train because there was nowhere to jump or run to. The small passage of tracks always made Smokey feel uneasy whenever he walked on it. It wasn't all that long ago when he had rescued Jacob from that very stretch. When that train came barreling down the tracks his life had flashed before his eyes. He put that thought out of his mind.

They entered the path to the tracks and began walking in the glimpses of sunshine that littered the railroad ties and danced on the rails. It was peaceful. The events of the night before almost seemed unreal, and the idea of Hans and his brothers chasing them seemed so far away.

Smokey's go-to hiding spot was a house that his band of friends, called the brothers, used as a sort of clubhouse for their Friday night card game. Now that they had started high school, the brothers didn't meet together as often as they had as inseparable middle schoolers. The house would be a good refuge where the boys could stay out of sight.

Smokey watched as Do What and Brent chatted together as they walked. Do What and Brent had hit it off the moment they met. Though they had an age gap, that didn't seem to bother either of them. They had similar interests and personalities. They spoke of deeper things than most people their age. They discussed segregation, politics, and the need for education reform. It was like hanging out with two pint-sized professors. Smokey didn't often engage in the conversation, but he did listen. He wanted to let them be in their own world. Smokey had a feeling that Brent was as odd among his peers as Do What was among his. Seeing all the joy that came from their philosophizing it was hard to fathom that just a few hours earlier Mike had shot at the captors.

Smokey led them on the tracks. He figured they had at least a twenty-minute walk before they would emerge at the clearing where the abandoned company mining house was located. Though he hadn't been there in months, he knew they would be able to sneak in the rear window, which they always left unlocked.

The breeze in the trees danced back and forth as they made their way down the tracks. The calm Sunday morning made them almost forget they were in trouble. All they had wanted to do was float the river and catch some fish. Now they were here running for their lives, hoping to find a way out. Smokey had an idea of how to get Hans and his brothers off their tail, and if he could pull it off, it might save Brent and get him back home safely. Smokey had a plan; the brothers, his group of friends, always said, if there was a way Smokey would figure it out. He was more confident when the plans didn't involve life and death. His clever way of thinking usually worked best if he was trying to get out of trouble from school, or how to sneak a jar of moonshine. This was a different matter entirely and he didn't want to let down Brent and Do What.

They made good time walking, and there was no sign of the train as they entered into the stretch of track that was walled by rock on both sides. Smokey bent down to hold onto the tracks to see if he could feel any vibration from a train that might be traveling in the distance. It was still, and he sighed in relief. He and Do What had escaped the train once before in a near miss and he didn't want to experience that again.

He rushed Do What and Brent past the stretch of inescapable track until they were once again in a spot that was not a trap. Do What seemed oblivious to the peril they could be in or even that they were in the very spot where they were almost killed once before. Smokey heard Brent and Do What talking about how the television had made a huge change on the way people saw things in the world. A topic, he was certain, that none of the brothers or people in the county would want to hear. TV was their escape if they owned one. Anyone who didn't have a TV spent all their time at the movie theatre in town. Smokey had never thought of television as being a bad thing at all. He loved it when he could get to a friend's house who had one.

They made it to the clearing of brush that led to the abandoned company house. They all proceeded with caution. Smokey told the boys to stay back and hide in the brush, that he needed to go get something. He left them crouching in the bushes and headed toward the small house of Mr. Wilson, who had a homestead just around the bend.

Mr. Wilson was in his eighties and was a fixture of the county. He wasn't a particularly social man. He preferred to be alone. When Smokey was a boy, there were urban legends that said he caught kids and cooked them in a stew. People believed he had a huge caldron in his house, used to cook kids down so he could grind their bones and use them as fertilizer for his garden. People said he cooked and ate his own family. Whether it was just urban legend or not, Smokey did not want to cross paths with Mr. Wilson; he just needed to borrow something from his yard.

Brent and Do What peered from behind the bushes, watching as Smokey disappeared around the bend. Do What knew of the legends about Mr. Wilson as well but thought it might be better if he kept that to himself; he didn't want to worry Brent with any ideas if he knew that Smokey was entering the yard of a legendary deranged killer of children. He thought it best if they just stayed put and didn't try to attract any unwarranted attention. Do What had seen Mr. Wilson on several occasions, mostly from afar. They had often dared each other to go to his yard and try to recover some item that would prove their valor and level up on their social barometer. Being able to say you made it in and out of Mr. Wilson's yard and survived was a badge of honor in Northfork.

One time, Smokey, Do What, and the gang of brothers were attempting to show their courage after a baseball game they played in an open field near the slate dump not far from the abandoned miner's house. Larry, who was older by a year, dared Smokey to sneak into Mr. Wilson's yard and ring the triangle that hung on the side of the pump where he drew water from a well. The triangle was probably there for when Mr. Wilson's family was still alive and he would call them in to eat supper. But the legend now said that the triangle was rung by Mr. Wilson when he had caught a child that he was going to cook in his stew. Everyone knew the sound of that triangle and often, even if they weren't anywhere near Mr. Wilson's house, people would flinch if they heard it. Smokey, who had never backed down from a dare, had taken the challenge and made his way to the yard where old man Wilson kept the triangle hanging. Smokey hadn't noticed that Mr. Wilson was still working in his garden behind his house. When Smokey snuck up to the triangle to declare his victory, Mr. Wilson was just steps away from him. Just as Smokey took the metal striker and began hitting it against the insides of the triangle, Mr. Wilson yelled at him in a stern voice.

"Hey, what are you doing in my yard?"

Smokey had frozen, too scared to even run. He had stared back at Mr. Wilson in awe and terror. Mr. Wilson looked agitated, his brow furrowed, as he raised his voice.

"I better not ever catch you in my yard again!"

The tone of Mr. Wilson's voice conveyed something much more threatening than his words. In Smokey's mind, Mr. Wilson would skin him alive and boil his young bones if he ever set foot back there again. Smokey finally got the courage to break away and run. He was as white as a ghost when he got back but was one of only a few that had ever made it into his yard to ring the triangle. He was talked about for months after. Whenever someone was missing or even gone for a long period of time, the brothers would say that they were taken by Mr. Wilson.

Mr. Wilson wore the same outfit every day: a dingy button-down shirt, a pair of bibbed overalls, and a straw hat that cast an eerie shadow on his face and made his leathery skin seem scarier. He would come to town sometimes but mostly got his groceries delivered by Ray, who ran the grocery store in Cinder Bottom. Even though Ray had seen him, he only really communicated with him on the telephone. He was instructed to leave the groceries on the porch.

Mr. Wilson was as real as anyone in the county but was one of its most feared and mysterious inhabitants. Some say that Mr. Wilson went mad when his entire family was killed in a fire when their house burned down some fifty years ago. Mr. Wilson was once a farmer that lived in North Carolina, not far from Shatley Springs. Shatley Springs was a place that was known for having spring water that had amazing healing properties. People traveled hundreds of miles to collect the water and return it to their homes to treat the sick and strengthen the weary. It was known as a magical place for hundreds of years. When Mr. Wilson lost his family, he moved to Northfork, vowing never to return. He had been a recluse ever since.

Do What and Smokey had grown a bit too old to believe in the old wives' tales but were still wary that Mr. Wilson might do something to anyone who snuck in his yard to "borrow something."

Smokey made his way as quiet as a church mouse toward Mr. Wilson's house. There was a series of small hedges that flanked his property and provided cover for sneaking closer without drawing any attention. Smokey didn't want to be seen, so he took his time, sometimes crawling on his hands and knees to avoid any chance of being detected.

The boys noticed Smokey popping up here and there but couldn't see him for long because he disappeared into the shrubs.

Once Smokey was close enough, he watched and waited to see if there were any signs of Mr. Wilson. Smokey thought that there was little chance that he would be working in the garden, because most folks didn't tend to their gardens on Sunday, the Lord's Day. But that didn't mean he wasn't sitting on his porch whittling or peeling apples from his tree.

Smokey stood still and studied the perimeter of the house. A window had a clear view of his yard. Smokey had always felt a strange connection to Mr. Wilson because he had kin that lived not far from Shatley Springs. Back when Smokey had escaped the old man's place last time, he had asked his father about Mr. Wilson and whether or not he had heard of his family there in North Carolina. His pa had said that they were a well-known family who were considered upright people. Ever since Mr. Wilson's family died, though, their clan had mostly vanished from conversation. Mr. Wilson supposedly still had family in North Carolina, but they didn't visit or communicate much with him. Smokey figured that they must have held him responsible for the family dying in the fire.

His pa said that Mr. Wilson was out working early in the fields one morning when the potbelly stove caught the house on fire. His family was still asleep and were trapped inside when the fire engulfed the tiny house. His wife narrowly escaped the giant flames and thick black smoke that billowed from the intense inferno. She dragged what was left of her burned body to the triangle that hung near the well and rang it as loud as she could until she gave out and collapsed onto the ground. Mr. Wilson, who heard the ringing, rushed home to find his house in flames and his wife lying lifeless in the yard. He held her for her last breaths and then she died. He tried to enter the house to save his children, but it was already too late. All the little ones inside had perished. He was grief-stricken, and from there on out he lived a life in solitude.

Smokey tried not to think about all of it as he made his way closer to Mr. Wilson's yard. He had already had one chance meeting of Mr. Wilson, and he didn't want to press his luck.

Mr. Wilson's house was an old hand-built log cabin. It was simple, basic, and rustic even for that part of the county. The subtle smoke of the fire rose from the chimney, and Smokey tried to remove the image of the infamous caldron hanging above it. He had to stay focused if he was going to help save Brent and get Hans and his brothers off his back.

He was about one hundred feet from the edge of Mr. Wilson's yard now, and his breath became heavy. He was sweating even though it was not warm outside. His clothes were still slightly damp from the river, and his sneakers still squeaked from the water inside his shoes. He didn't want to be there, but this was the only way he could get Brent out of this situation. He hoped it worked because if it didn't, they might all end up in the stew.

Smokey waited for several minutes to make sure the coast was clear. Maybe Mr. Wilson was gone. His truck was nowhere in sight, and Smokey hoped he had headed to Bluefield for the day, or at least would be gone for a few minutes longer, that's all he needed to get what he was after. When Smokey was confident that there was no sign of Mr. Wilson, he made his move and headed to the yard.

Do What and Brent could see Smokey now as he jogged across the yard. Do What instinctively grabbed Brent's shoulder, nervously watching Smokey. Brent turned and gave him a look. The kind of look that says, "What they heck are you doing and what's going on?" Smokey was now halfway to the house.

"What's he doing?" Brent whispered.

Do What held his finger to his lips, and they continued to watch Smokey inch his way closer to the house. Do What wondered what he was after in Mr. Wilson's yard that would be worth getting caught. Maybe there was a secret gun stash or something that would protect them from Hans and his brothers.

Smokey inched his way even closer to the house. He was determined to get what he needed. He knew he probably only had one shot to get what he was after, and then he would have to run. He drew closer to the well where Mr. Wilson pumped his water each day and evening. Mr. Wilson didn't have any running water in his house, and the pump was the spot where the triangle hung.

He was just a few feet away from the pump when he heard a rumbling from an old truck. Mr. Wilson was pulling up to the front of the house!

Do What and Brent stared at Smokey, trying to wave to get his attention to alert him of Mr. Wilson, but they didn't want to risk shouting for him.

Smokey froze, like a deer caught in the headlights of a car speeding down the road. He heard the tires rolling over the gravel. He was afraid that the sound of his heart beating in his chest might give his location away. His hands were on the triangle now, and he gently lifted it off the hook where it hung and slowly began to back away. He kept an eye on the corner of the truck, which was visible only partially from the back of the house. His slow movements turned into a sprint, and he headed back to Do What and Brent. Just as Mr. Wilson was rounding the back porch to put away some of his groceries, Smokey dove into the bushes out of sight. The bushes moved while a strong wind blew, and the leaves rustled. Mr. Wilson looked over in the direction of their hiding place but didn't see anything. He proceeded into the house, closing the door with a slam.

Do What and Brent tried not to gasp at the amazing dive into the bushes and Smokey's near miss with Mr. Wilson. They were relieved but confused. Why was Smokey willing to risk his life to get a triangle?

"Smokey, what the hell you gonna do with that?" Do What asked.

"I aim to use it if I need to. Now come on, let's go before he realizes the triangle is missing," Smokey ordered.

Do What wondered what Smokey meant by "use it if he needed to." They all snuck backwards toward the train tracks to head down another path that led to the abandoned miner's house.

At one point, there had been a whole row of these houses. Over the years, their numbers had decreased one by one as they were sold, burnt down, or, like this one, abandoned. The coal companies had built houses for miners who worked in the nearby mines.

It required the miners to pay rent to the company as well as buy groceries at the company store. Once you were working in the mines, it was hard to get out. Your house was owned by the company, your paycheck was sent as credit to the company store, and even if you wanted to, there weren't many jobs that paid as much as the mines did. Though the coal mines and railroad had built up places like Welch and Bluefield into large cities for the area, it was not as bustling as it once had been. The need for coal after the war had shifted, and the use of oil for power had increased.

The people of West Virginia had a deep respect for the coal deposits, and yet the conditions in the mines meant miners rarely lived long or healthy lives. Most developed black lung, were injured, or just got beat up by the grueling work. They were willing to work, though, in order to take care of their families. Their dedication meant that even those without an education got to live a decent life.

When Do What's dad was injured in the mines, it had been a big blow to his family. His brother, Mike, had dropped out of high school, even though he had been a tremendous athlete and a good student. He had gone to work in the mines since his father could no longer work, which made their father resent Mike in a strange way. Their father had not taken this fact well. While some saw it as a blessing that Mike could work in the mines, he saw it as a curse and a reminder about how incapable he was to provide for his family.

His drinking got worse when the pain from his injury became unbearable, and he took out his frustration mainly on Mike. Do What stayed clear of his dad but often took a beating as well. Do What never had a bad thing to say about his father, even after a beating. He just picked himself up and kept going.

When they were far enough away from Mr. Wilson's house, Brent asked Smokey, "Where are we going?"

Smokey pointed to the abandoned house. Do What was feeling a little apprehensive. Though they had snuck into the house many times and used it as a hideout for the gang of brothers to play cards and drink, they had some trouble there the year before, and his mind had not been prepared to return to the house with another challenging situation. The house had once been a nice home, but over the years it was starting to show its age. At this point, it looked like one strong wind might blow it over one day.

They made their way to the back of the house where an unlocked kitchen window served as their entrance to the hideout. Hans and his brothers would never find them there, and it would give Smokey a chance to think through his plan. Do What rarely questioned Smokey, but he was a bit confused as to what they might do next.

"Smokey, you figure those boys have given up and drove on?" Do What asked.

Smokey was getting a small log that he used as a step stool to get up to the window of the house. He turned to Do What.

"I doubt they've given up," Smokey said.

If they asked enough people, they could figure out who Smokey and Do What were and that they lived in the area. Smokey didn't want to take the chance that they might find Brent. He seemed so frail and innocent. Smokey felt sorry for Brent, not just because he was kidnapped but because he was probably picked on at school as well. Brent was the kind of kid that Smokey would have picked on when he was younger, calling him names like sissy and teasing him for not being good at sports.

Smokey was sent home from school once for putting a younger boy in a tree hanging from his underwear for all of the school to see. The gang of brothers had dared him, and he thought it might be funny. It had been funny to everyone except the boy, named Sean. They called him Precious because of his more delicate nature. He was humiliated and stopped going to school after that day. He went to live with his family in South Carolina, and, last anyone had heard, he hadn't spoken since that day. His family thought he got ill and became mute, but Smokey knew it was his fault for hanging him by his underwear from a tree. That had been the last straw, and the kid just broke. Smokey felt bad but had no way of finding the boy to say he was sorry.

Do What heaved Smokey up to the window ledge, where he pried the window open. He was relieved to see it was still unlocked. Next, Do What had Brent steady himself on the stump and lifted him up to the window. He looked like a newborn puppy who had no idea how to use his legs. He twisted and turned as he wiggled his way through the window. Do What was able to almost leap into the window and fell with a thud onto the floor.

Smokey looked for the small kerosene lantern that they had hidden along with some kitchen matches. Though it was light out, the boards on many of the windows made it dark inside. Do What found a large bucket that he turned over for a seat and offered it to Brent. Do What grabbed a small, hand-woven stool to sit on.

Smokey held the large triangle tight to his chest and paced back and forth in the living room area as the other two watched him and waited. Do What had seen Smokey like this before and knew better than to interrupt him when he was deep in thought. It was best to let him share when he was ready. Do What had retrieved a small card table, wobbly but still functional, and a used deck of cards and handed them to Brent to deal.

"Are we going to play pinochle?" Brent asked.

Do What chuckled and took the stack to deal the cards.

"We are playing Five Card Stud, deuces wild," Do What proclaimed.

Brent picked up the cards as if they were alien rocks. He had never played poker and had no idea what wild deuces had to do with it. Do What explained the game to him and how the wild cards work. He wanted to be sure that Brent understood before they began. Do What always took the time to explain things before he started them; he didn't want anyone to get it wrong. Maybe it was because his father always told him that he ain't ever done nothin' right in his whole life.

Smokey continued to pace back and forth, clutching the iron triangle. He had an idea, but he needed a plan, one that wouldn't get them killed or put Brent in anymore jeopardy than he already was. Brent and Do What continued to play cards until Smokey declared he had to go out and do something. The boys got up from the rickety card table to follow him back out the window.

"You two stay here. Do What, keep Brent out of sight and stay inside," Smokey said firmly.

Do What nodded and they sat back down to continue playing cards. Smokey made his way out the window, almost forgetting he was clutching the triangle, his hands turning white from the tight grip. He laid the triangle next to the log he used as a step stool and headed into the bushes to make his way to see a friend in Cinder Bottom. His friend Lorenzo operated the boarding house just on the inside of town. He needed to get there fast, and he considered taking the tracks to get back but didn't think he had time.

He snuck back along the bushes toward Mr. Wilson's house and looked to see if the coast was clear. There was no sign of Mr. Wilson on the porch, so he crept around the hedges and made his way to the front of the house. From the corner of his eye, he saw Mr. Wilson in the distance working in the garden on the far end of his property. He made his way undetected past Mr. Wilson's well where the triangle had hung and then to the front of the house. He stuttered for a moment but then made his way to the driver's side door of Mr. Wilson's pickup.

Most old-timers often left the keys in the sun visor, which is what Smokey was counting on. When he climbed into the cab and closed the door behind him, he reached toward the visor and held his breath, hoping he had been right. With a quick tug, the visor unfolded from the ceiling, and the keys fell onto his lap. He knew he might get in some real trouble taking Mr. Wilson's truck, but he had no other choice. If his plan was to work, he had to get to town quickly. Lorenzo could help, but Smokey knew he had to get there before he left for lunch.

Not only had Smokey stolen the triangle, but he was now stealing his truck. He planned to return it, of course, but he needed to get to town quick. He just hoped he didn't give Mr. Wilson a heart attack when he realized what he had done.

Smokey slowly turned the key to the truck and hoped that it didn't make much noise. It was an older 1939 Ford truck, but it was kept in great condition. This was partially due to the fact that Mr. Wilson rarely went anywhere, but also because, like his garden, Mr. Wilson kept his vehicle well tended to.

When the engine turned over it almost purred, which relieved Smokey. He put it in gear, backed up, and turned the truck in the direction of Cinder Bottom. He drove off and looked in his rearview mirror for any sign of Mr. Wilson, but he saw nothing. With any luck he could get to town and return to the miner's house before he even knew the truck was gone.

He drove fast but didn't want to draw too much attention to himself, so he put on the straw hat left on the passenger's seat. Mr. Wilson wore the hat low over his eyes when he went to his outings in Bluefield or Welch. Smokey pulled the brim of the hat down to keep a low profile hoping he would not be noticed. He had about ten minutes before he would be at Lorenzo's place.

CHAPTER
8

As Smokey headed toward town, Lorenzo was dusting his collection of opera and classical music, humming and dancing along to one of his favorite sonatas. He rather enjoyed Sunday mornings because it was usually quiet at the boarding house.

He had grown up there. His mother had fled Italy during the first World War and started hosting travelers when he was just a young boy. He had inherited the business when his parents died. A beautiful picture of his mother hung over the front desk near the collection of records.

Lorenzo had never married and was a respected man in Cinder Bottom, but he stayed to himself most of the time. The decor of the office was reminiscent of another time. His mother had brought just a few items with her when she fled, but the room felt like an Italian parlor from the turn of the century.

The music played and Lorenzo swayed as he dusted. He had just finished his last cup of coffee and was getting ready to close the office to take his lunch as he did every Sunday afternoon.

Hans and his brothers pulled up to the parking lot of Lorenzo's boarding house, one of the first places of business they encountered when they rolled into town. The eldest brother, Frank, jumped out of the driver's side and told the others to stay. He motioned for Hans to follow him, and they entered the office door, the bell sounding their arrival.

Lorenzo turned and with the most pleasant tone, welcomed them as he lowered the music.

"Welcome," Lorenzo said but quickly realized the boys were not there to rent a room. His face turned a little less friendly when he noticed the knife attached to the waist of the older brother. "Can I help you?" he asked.

"We're looking for somebody," Frank said in a stern voice. He stepped toward Lorenzo with a tinge of rage in his eyes while Hans stayed close to the door, almost blocking the entrance.

"Is that so?" Lorenzo asked. He turned the music off now and made his way behind the front desk. "Who are you looking for?"

"Couple of boys stole something from me, and I'm looking to get it back," Frank said in a forced polite voice.

"That's a shame that someone took something from you," Lorenzo said. His hand gently rested on the desk behind the counter. He spoke while slowly opening the desk drawer where a pistol was stored for emergencies and unruly guests.

Cinder Bottom was a place where people could come and be anonymous and do things like drink, gamble, or be with prostitutes, and no one would mention your name or remember you if you wanted to be forgotten. It was obvious to him that these boys didn't understand the nature of Cinder Bottom, and he wasn't going to let them push him around.

"We're looking for a boy named Smokey and his friend, about this tall," the boy said. He held his hand up just under his nose to indicate the height of Do What, who was taller than Smokey.

Lorenzo nodded, contemplating the description.

"Have you seen them?" he asked.

"A Smokey, you said? That's the name?" He scratched his head rather convincingly. "No, I have not seen a Smokey."

The boy scowled trying to see if there was any deception in his reply. He stared for a long second. "Well, if you see him, tell him I'm looking for him."

"Sure, what's your name?" Lorenzo asked.

"He'll know who we are," the boy said and slowly backed up to the door and snapped to have Hans open it. They both turned and walked out. They all piled back into the truck and made their way down the road.

Lorenzo came from behind the desk and peeked out the window to see if they were gone. He grabbed his hat and coat and placed a sign that read, "Closed for Lunch" on the door. He quickly made his way down the sidewalk toward the main part of town.

When Smokey arrived at Lorenzo's place, he pulled into the alley behind the building in order to park the truck out of sight. He made his way around the back of the office and toward the front door. There was no sign of Hans and his brother, and that gave Smokey a little relief.

When he got to the door, he saw the "Closed for Lunch" sign. He had missed Lorenzo, but he knew that there was a spare key to the office hidden in the geranium pot near the front step. Smokey grabbed the key and showed himself in, making sure he wasn't seen. He looked around to be certain that Lorenzo wasn't there and then went behind the counter of the main desk. He opened the drawer, and there was the pistol. Smokey stared and looked again toward the door. He grabbed the gun and tucked it into his waist under his damp, weathered, dirty shirt. He eased the drawer closed and made his way back toward the office door.

He heard a car pull up and a door shut. He peaked out the window to see who it was. It was a fancy black car, a Lincoln Continental. A man in a black suit stepped out, put his cap on, and walked around to the passenger side. He opened the door and a tall man in a blue suit stepped out. The driver closed the door behind him.

"Wait here, James," the man said to the driver and walked toward the office door.

Smokey hadn't locked it, but the sign read, "Closed for Lunch." He hoped that this might deter him. When the man came closer to the door and was able to read the sign, he paused. Then with his hand on the doorknob, he tried to peek in the window.

Smokey ducked and was narrowly missed being seen. Smokey knelt, almost frozen, hoping the man wouldn't open the door. His heart was pounding, and he didn't even want to breathe. The man stared for a long time, studying the office, then turned and walked back down the stairs and motioned for the driver to open the door.

"We will come back after lunch," the man said. The driver closed the door, and they drove away.

Smokey's heart was beating so fast it was as if he had just run all the way from the miner's house. He exhaled with a sigh of relief. He regained his composure after about a minute once he was certain that the car had driven away. He slowly stood to look out the window. He wanted to make sure the black Lincoln was gone. He peered through the window of the office door and standing there, staring directly back at him, was Frank.

Smokey ducked down in terror, hoping what he saw was just his imagination. There was no movement on the other side of the door, and Smokey wondered if being sleep-deprived had contributed to a hallucination. He breathed deeply but didn't hear the doorknob move nor any sounds outside. He slowly stood to his feet and peeked outside, but there was no one standing on the other side of the door. Smokey shook his head to clear his mind and felt the cold steel of the pistol pushing against his waist. He pulled his shirt down to make sure the weapon was concealed. He felt a little guilty taking Lorenzo's pistol, but he figured that he would understand under the circumstances.

With the coast clear, Smokey slowly opened the door, stepped out on to the porch, and pulled the door closed behind him. That's when they seized him. Hans and his brother sprung from one side of the door and grabbed Smokey by the arms.

"We gotcha, you little weasel," Hans said, grinning and laughing. They looked around to make sure no one was watching them as they put Smokey into the cab of the truck. Hans sat on Smokey's right. Frank jumped into the driver's seat, put it into gear, and drove off.

"Where is he?" Frank asked.

Smokey was tight-lipped. He faced forward, not saying a word.

"Frank wants answers," Hans said, prodding Smokey in the side.

Up till this point, Smokey hadn't even known the older brother's name. He immediately became fixated on finding a connection to Frank in his memory vault. Like his Ma, Smokey kept a running list of names, kinfolk, and any known reputational points be they respected and revered for their acts of goodwill or be they unspoken for their misdeeds or troubles at home. Who the heck was Frank? Smokey's mind was spinning with the question.

Frank stared intently down the road and waited for Smokey to respond. Smokey contemplated saying nothing, but considering the situation, he figured he needed to at least give them some answer.

"What do you want him for?" Smokey asked.

Hans slapped Smokey upside his head and made his blood boil. Smokey gritted his teeth as he sucked in a deep breath of air into his lungs. His rib cage expanded and as his mind raced with rage he felt the cold steel of the pistol against his waist. Smokey was tempted to go for it, but knew he better keep his head cool and keep the gun out of sight.

"You ain't asking the questions," Hans said, poking Smokey in the ribs even harder this time. "Answer him."

Smokey took a shallow breath and calculated what to say. He wanted to punch Hans in the face for stealing his fish, for holding him hostage in the cabin, and for taking Brent. He had beat up boys for less, but he was outnumbered and needed to buy some time.

"He's behind Geneva's restaurant waiting for me to return," Smokey said.

"Good boy," Frank said, and started up the road toward Geneva's. Geneva's was only a short drive away, so Smokey didn't have long to think. When they got to the restaurant, Smokey directed them to pull around the back near the kitchen, where Jerome had fed them just a few hours earlier. The truck came to a halt, and Hans and Frank stared at him.

"Where is he?" Frank demanded. Smokey stirred in his seat and then pointed to the kitchen door.

"In there," Smokey said. "I'll go get him." He urged Hans to open the door. Hans didn't budge. Smokey gave him a glare.

"Do you want me to get him or not?" Smokey said. He stared into Hans's eyes and for the first time realized how young he was. He might have been the same age as Smokey, but his mentality came across as if he were a much younger, more naïve boy. He figured he was just trying to do what his brother would approve of.

"Let him out," Frank commanded.

Hans jumped out and let Smokey slide out of the bench seat of the truck.

"Go with him, Hans," Frank said.

Smokey looked at him but realized it would be pointless to argue. He walked up the steps toward the kitchen. The screen door was shut, and there was a great deal of commotion as the restaurant handled the lunch rush. Smokey walked slowly up the steps, looking back at Frank, who was pointing for him to continue on. Hans walked so close behind him he was almost on his heels.

"Stand here for a second. I need to get Jerome's attention," Smokey said, gesturing for Hans to step to the side where he wouldn't be visible from the kitchen. Smokey stood just in sight of the kitchen, took his hands, and placed them on his lips to make a small cuplike shape. He created a whistle sound that sounded like a bird. Hans stared at Smokey, then turned back towards the truck to get affirmation that he was doing the right thing. Frank nodded his approval, and Hans turned his attention back to Smokey. He gave the low whistle a second time, and within moments Jerome arrived at the door.

"Jerome, it's me, Smokey," he said in a hushed voice. "I'm here to get the boy."

Jerome looked at him, then at the truck, and then back to Smokey.

"Smokey, wait here for a minute," he said, leaving the two waiting on the porch.

Hans stared at Smokey suspiciously and then glanced back at his brother. Smokey waited with bated breath, not knowing what Jerome might be up to. Jerome seemed to have understood that he was using their secret signal. Smokey trusted Jerome with his life. Next to Ray at the grocery store and Lorenzo, Jerome was one of his most trusted friends in Cinder Bottom.

Jerome had been only a boy when he made his way from Charlotte, North Carolina, to Cinder Bottom. He was kicked out of his house because his father said his son was soft and a sissy, that he dishonored his name because he wasn't a real man.

At thirteen, Jerome left home and hitchhiked to Cinder Bottom. He wasn't sure why he came there, but he had heard that you could be anything you wanted in Cinder, and he wanted to make a life on his own. Geneva had given him a job as a dishwasher, and he had worked his way up to cook. He was a hard worker and one of the kindest people Smokey had ever met.

He was almost twenty now, but he had the wisdom of someone twice his age. They had agreed on their secret whistle when Smokey had gotten into some trouble before and needed help. Jerome told him to use the signal if he ever found himself in a pickle and that he would do his best to help him out. Smokey hoped that, somehow, Jerome would know what to do.

Smokey was out of good ideas and was counting on Jerome to get him out of this crazy situation.

Smokey could sense Hans was growing irritated by the way he looked back at Frank, who was scowling at them both. Smokey peered into the door to see if he could see Jerome, but there was just the regular commotion of a busy Sunday afternoon.

It seemed like an eternity waiting for Jerome to return. He finally reappeared, poking his head out from behind the screen door, wearing his paper hat. He handed Smokey a piece of paper and whispered something quietly too low for Hans to hear before he closed the door and returned to the kitchen. Hans rushed to Smokey to see what the note said and more importantly to ask what Jerome had said.

"What did he say?" Hans asked.

Smokey stared at the note and then looked at Hans.

"He told me the boy ran off," Smokey said.

Hans wasn't satisfied. He wanted to know what the note said. He didn't trust Smokey. He grabbed the note from his hand and opened it. It read, "You owe $1.80." Hans looked at him and Smokey shrugged.

"I guess he must of ate and ran," Smokey said.

"Where'd he run off to?" Hans asked.

Smokey looked at him, also a bit confused by the note. "I dunno. He just said he ran off and handed me this note."

Hans stared at the note as if it were ancient Egyptian hieroglyphics. They both made their way back down the porch. Smokey's mind once again went to the cold steel of the gun in his waistband. For a brief second, he thought about pulling it out and raising it to aim straight at Hans. But Smokey knew that Frank probably had his rifle right by his side, waiting for any trouble.

Smokey was reluctant to move forward. Maybe he could run off and head down the alley to Big Ma's place. Hopefully they were all up getting ready for their Sunday gathering. They would be setting up the card table out back and preparing the fire to grill the chicken and pieces of pork for their weekly affair. But at this point, Smokey had already indirectly involved Lorenzo and now Jerome. He didn't want to draw any more people into this situation, especially with Brent and Do What still unaware of what had happened to Smokey.

Smokey followed Hans to the truck but stood and paused as he approached the open door. Hans motioned for him to get in, but he stood his ground.

Hans relayed to Frank what Jerome had said. He handed over the note as well. Frank studied the note, then scowled at Smokey, who stood just an arm's length away from Hans. Frank was growing impatient and looked at both of them like they were idiots.

"Where's the boy?" Frank asked Smokey.

"Don't know exactly, but I have an idea," Smokey said. He motioned for Hans to scoot over so he could sit near the door. "I'll tell you where to drive." Smokey continued looking at Frank as if to say, "You gotta trust me. What choice do you have?"

Frank finally nodded but kept a suspicious eye on Smokey as he climbed into the truck. He threw one arm over the back of the seat and reversed the truck out of the parking lot.

Smokey pointed up the road, "There's an old moonshine still up that way. We use it sometimes as a hiding place." He wanted to make sure to sell the lie so he continued, "We keep rations and a dry place to sit and an old stove to cook and keep warm."

Frank was skeptical. Nevertheless, he put the truck into gear and they lurched forward towards Burke Holler.

The boys headed up the narrow road between the hills, sliding back and forth on the truck's bench seat as Frank sped around each curve of the road. Smokey could still feel the cold steel of the pistol and tried not to think about wanting to aim the gun at Frank. Smokey wasn't typically a violent kid, but these were not normal circumstances.

"What do you want with the kid, anyway?" Smokey asked.

Frank didn't turn to look at him. Instead, he stared steadily ahead, his mouth closed tightly. Hans, on the other hand, blurted out the truth.

"That lil' twerp's daddy is the boss over the broke down mine that 'bout near killed our pa," Hans spewed with rage. Frank turned and gave a look to Hans, clearly indicating if he knew what was good for him he better shut his big mouth.

"Don't you worry about why we want the kid," he said, looking over at Smokey. "Just give him to us and mind your own damned business. Stay out of it and you won't get hurt."

Smokey was relieved to finally understand why they were after Brent. Do What's brother Mike also held a grudge against the big wigs of the mine who had been in charge when his father was crushed and almost killed by a mine explosion. Sometimes, when Mike got especially drunk, he would lash out in a rage, vowing to kill that man who was responsible for his father's injuries. Though the president had already left the company, Mike hadn't forgotten what he did to his dad, his family, and his future. Mining is a dangerous job, and everyone knew of the risks, but blaming the man in charge gave a direction to their anger.

Smokey sat quietly and listened but knew that this was not about money, it was about revenge. If they found Brent, they would use him as leverage to get back at his father and even hurt him. Smokey didn't know what had happened in the mines that had caused this anguish and pain in Frank and his brothers, but for a moment he had compassion for them.

Smokey's dad had worked in the mines since he left the farm in North Carolina and walked to West Virginia to make a better life for himself. The mines had provided for their family and given them a new life, but it was slowly taking the life away from his pa. The hard work and coal dust was taking a toll on his father. He could see him slowing down a little more every year. As Smokey watched his father get worn down, it strengthened his resolve to get out of McDowell County and find a life for himself outside the mines. He would make it out and see the world with Do What if he could ever convince him to go.

The truck had made its way up the holler now, and Smokey spotted a small spring ahead. It was hidden to most people, but Smokey had a practiced eye. He knew that wherever there was a supply of water, there was a chance of finding a moonshine still. He and the band of brothers hunted stills for fun. He had found this particular shine operation before it was abandoned. He had watched as the Feds raided and seized hundreds of gallons of liquor before destroying all the working parts of the still. The location was mostly hidden by the curve of the land and a thick row of rhododendron bushes that obscured the site. Smokey and the band of brothers had used what was left behind as a hideout when the weather was good before they discovered the abandoned miner's house.

There was a small patch of dirt on the side of the road, and Smokey instructed Frank to park there.

When they pulled off the road, Frank gave Smokey a scowl.

"The boy better be here," he said to Smokey.

Smokey nodded reassuringly but felt his anxiety rising. He still didn't have a plan.

"They're probably up that holler," Smokey said, pointing in the direction of the still.

Hans looked at Frank and then at his other brothers in the back of the pickup. He motioned for them to go check it out. Smokey grabbed the handle of the door, and Frank stopped him.

"You stay here," he said.

The other brothers headed up the holler. Smokey knew it was about a fifteen minute walk up and back. That would buy him some time to figure out what to say when they discovered they weren't there.

Hans, Frank, and Smokey sat in silence for what seemed like an eternity. Smokey had almost forgotten that he had taken Old Man Wilson's truck and could only imagine how mad he was when he discovered it missing. He wondered how Do What and Brent were getting along. He figured as long as they stayed inside, they would be fine.

Frank began to bounce his right leg, which rocked the entire cab of the truck. He was obviously feeling anxious. He opened the door to get out.

"Stay here and watch him," Frank said to Hans. Frank exited the truck and pulled out a cigarette to light. He searched his pockets for a book of matches but couldn't find them. Smokey took out his lighter and handed it out the window to Frank. Frank stared, skeptical, seeming to weigh whether it was worth defiling his cigarette with Smokey's lighter. But, with no other option, he took it, lit his cigarette, and tossed the lighter back in Smokey's lap.

Frank walked up to the front bumper and rested his foot on the chrome, taking a long slow drag. He stared off into the distance in the direction of where his brothers had gone. He seemed lost in thought. Smokey wondered what he was thinking and how he might be planning his next move if he did find Brent. Would he take him for ransom, or was he gonna torture him or trap him down in an old mine shaft to die a slow painful death? How did he plan to take out his vengeance on Brent's father? Smokey was uncertain but knew he had to get Brent back home.

Hans kept his eyes fixed up the holler like Frank. He pretended Smokey wasn't even there. Smokey thought he would take advantage of the moment to see what information he could get from Hans.

"So, what do y'all want to do with the boy?" Smokey said. He turned to look at Hans and see if he was willing to take the bait.

"You don't wanna know," Hans said. He seemed a bit frightened by his own statement, which made Smokey think maybe they had more planned than he had suspected.

"Y'all sure are going through a lot of trouble for some boy," Smokey said.

"He ain't just some boy," Hans said. His posture shifted as he spoke.

"Well, I ain't sure he's worth it. I mean, he's just a kid," Smokey said.

"He ain't just some kid. He's the son of Marty Ferguson, and he's worth a lot of money," Hans blurted out.

Smokey could tell Hans wanted to talk so he nodded, hoping he could encourage him to go on.

"That kid's the heir to a huge fortune, and we aim to get some, if not all, of it," Hans proclaimed. Smokey knew that this was about way more than just the money. These boys wanted revenge, and something told him that Frank wanted more. He wanted to make Brent's father suffer.

Smokey didn't say another word.

A moment later, Frank pulled his bottom lip and made a loud whistle to signal his brothers. They replied with another long whistle. Frank must have understood the signal, because he climbed back into the cab and started the truck. Soon, they saw the boys come running down the holler.

Smokey knew they had found nothing and was trying to figure out his next move. He kept thinking about the note that Jerome handed him. Why did he give him a note saying he owed $1.80? Smokey knew that Do What and Brent hadn't been back to Geneva's, and even if they had been, there was no way they owed that much money. What was Jerome trying to tell him? Smokey churned the words from the note in his mind but couldn't think of what it meant.

The boys came rushing down the ravine, whooping and hollering. As they jumped back into the bed of the truck, Frank turned to Smokey in disdain.

"Where are they?" Frank demanded. He grabbed Smokey by the collar and stared into his eyes, looking for answers. Smokey stared back in contemplation, then it hit him.

"I know where they went. There is only one place left to hide just outside Cinder Bottom," Smokey said.

"And where is that?" Frank said, losing his patience. Smokey instructed him to turn around and head back into town. He told him not to stop in Cinder but instead to keep driving to Northfork, back towards the miner's house where Smokey had left his friends. Smokey had an idea about what the note meant and desperately hoped he was right. Otherwise, he knew he was leading Hans and the boys straight for Do What and Brent.

Frank drove like a bat out of hell headed towards Cinder Bottom. The brothers squealed and whooped from the back of the truck as the tires on the pickup skidded with each turn in the winding road. Smokey was counting on him speeding, in hopes of attracting the attention of Sheriff Donnie.

They sped through Cinder without even a soul noticing them. Folks were too busy enjoying their Sunday afternoon to pay any attention to a truck speeding down the road.

When they whizzed past Lorenzo's boarding house, Smokey leaned forward to see if Mr. Wilson's truck was still sitting in the alley. The truck was parked right where he had left it. The sign still hung in Lorenzo's window: "Closed for Lunch." He had wished that he had snuck out before Frank, Hans, and his brothers had found him. He then thought of the pistol. He had fired a pistol several times. He was a pretty good shot, but he wasn't a murderer.

Smokey knew he was out of options. If he stalled too long, they would certainly find a way to make him talk. He hoped that Brent and Do What had already left the miner's house. Once Old Man Wilson discovered his truck missing, he would have gone snooping around, looking for anyone who might have seen anything. Maybe Do What and Brent were spooked by Mr. Wilson. If not, Smokey hoped they would hear the truck coming when he and the boys rolled up the gravel driveway. He hoped they would manage to escape back out from the window they'd snuck in through earlier. Smokey started to feel like a traitor, but he had to stick with his gut and trust his instincts.

Smokey had seen the look on Jerome's face; he had been serious and to the point. Also, there had been a certain look to the handwriting that he couldn't place. He wanted to examine the note again, but Frank had tossed it on the floor of the truck.

As the truck rolled into Northfork, Smokey could see the road that turned off towards the house. He instructed Frank to turn down the road that led to the railroad tracks and Mr. Wilson's house. There was smoke rising from the chimney of his house and Smokey thought of the stew pot and the tales of Mr. Wilson. He wondered for a moment if Brent and Do What were in the pot. He knew the tale wasn't true, but something about Mr. Wilson still terrified him.

When they neared the house, Smokey told Frank to pull around the side away from Mr. Wilson's house, where they could park unseen. He worried that Mr. Wilson saw him take his truck and was just waiting to catch him and toss him into the stew.

He tried to quiet his mind, but the ordeal of the last twenty-four hours flooded his thoughts. He wasn't certain of anything in this moment. Smokey had returned to the miner house because the note from Jerome had read, "You owe $1.80." Smokey had interpreted that to mean he needed to make a 180-degree turn and head back to where he had begun. He wasn't sure how he knew this, but nothing else made sense. He had started at the miner house, so he figured he would go back there. He wasn't certain that he was doing the right thing. What if he was wrong? What if he had led them right to Brent?

Smokey told Frank to park the truck and wait for a bit to be certain that no one saw them driving up. Minutes passed and Frank grew impatient. He motioned for them to get out.

"They better be in there." Frank snapped, pointing to the boarded-up house. Smokey nodded, and he and Hans jumped out of the truck. Smokey led the way with Hans following close behind him. Frank commanded the rest of the boys to stay in the back of the truck and keep a low profile. They obeyed and sat down low in the bed of the truck. They were dirty and undoubtedly tired, but they followed orders like little soldiers.

CHAPTER
9

Smokey motioned for Hans and Frank to follow him around the back of the house so they could get in through the window. Smokey moved the log that was used as a step stool close to the window so they could enter the house. The triangle fell against the house when he moved the stump. He hoped when they got inside, that Brent and Do What would be long gone. They may have left the card table and their makeshift chairs in place, but otherwise there should be no trace of them.

Smokey stood at the log and signaled for Hans to go first. Hans shook his head and refused. Frank pointed to Smokey to go first, so he stood on the log and leapt into the open window. He landed with a thud.

The room was dark. The small flicker of the lantern still burned but it was dim, and he couldn't tell if there was anyone in the room. Smokey thought he would call out to see if they were still there, but it was too late to forewarn them anyhow. Hans and Frank had already tumbled in behind him.

Smokey led them slowly toward the living room, where he had left Do What and Brent. The table was there; the cards lay on the tabletop and the soft glow of the lantern dimly lit the room.

The musty smell of the cabin filled their noses, and with each footstep, the floor creaked beneath them. Smokey was reminded of the fact that the house was abandoned because it had been condemned. The floor had evidence of termites. The paint peeled from the walls. Cobwebs hung everywhere. He had never stopped to see just how badly the house was falling apart.

As he surveyed the room, he saw no sign of his friends. Where had they gone? Smokey sure hoped they made it out of the house. Maybe they had made it to the train tracks and were headed back to Cinder Bottom.

When Frank entered the living room and saw the table, lantern, and cards, he turned to Smokey.

"Where did they go?" he grumbled. "You better not be leading us on some kinda wild goose chase."

Hans stood behind him, arms folded in equal defiance. The room was empty, but it was obvious that someone had been there recently. Frank instructed Hans to search the rest of the house to see if they were hiding in some cupboard or closet.

Frank then turned to Smokey, walked up to him, and stared him in the eye with a menacing look. Smokey stared right back, unwilling to fold to his posturing. Smokey was stalling, holding his gaze without flinching.

Hans returned, out of breath.

"No sign of them," he said.

"Where the hell did they go?" Frank said in a stern voice.

Smokey looked at him and then slowly scanned all around the room. "Maybe they just evaporated?" he said, without even the hint of a grin, which made Frank twitch with frustration.

"I don't want to ask you again," Frank said, grabbing Smokey by the arm.

Smokey tried to pull away, but Frank reached into his back pocket and pulled out his switchblade. He pointed the tip of the sharp blade at Smokey's face.

Smokey's face went hot, and he felt the cold barrel in his waistband push against his body. He had thought he might take the opportunity to show Frank that he was the one with the upper hand, but instead he kept his cool. He didn't want to hurt anyone, but if he had to choose between him and Frank, he would have no choice but to pull the gun from its hiding place and aim it right between his eyes.

Hans moved closer, and Frank stared intently into Smokey's eyes.

"I bet they ran to Old Man Wilson's house when they heard us driving around the back of this place," Smokey blurted out. He had hoped he sounded convincing even though he knew there was no way they would run there. "I'll go look," he said, walking past Frank's raised knife and past Hans.

Frank put his arm out to stop him.

"No chance. You wait here. I'll go look," Frank said. "Hans, you stay here and watch him. Don't let him out of your sight."

He handed Hans the knife, who grabbed it with pleasure and held his arm straight out, aiming it at Smokey like he was Errol Flynn getting ready for a sword fight. Smokey snickered as Frank went to walk out the front door.

Frank struggled to pry the door open. The house had settled, leaving the doors wedged and stuck in their frames. Frank pulled the door with all his might and it popped open to reveal it had been boarded up from the outside. He contemplated ripping the boards out one at a time but opted to head back to the kitchen and out the window.

Once Frank made his way out the back, Hans stared at Smokey and began to circle him. The soft flicker of the lantern created light that danced around their faces. Smokey didn't move, but watched

Hans circle around him. He felt his body heat up and watched Hans's every move.

"I think I should pay you back for losing my fish," Hans said.

He stepped behind Smokey and held the cold steel blade close to his neck. Smokey's blood began to boil. It was Hans who had stolen his fish, the biggest smallmouth bass in the Greenbrier River. Right then he had the mind to pull out that pistol and aim it right at Hans. He wanted to make him beg for mercy. Smokey despised him and wanted revenge more than anything. For a moment he forgot about Do What and Brent. All he could think about was how Hans stole the fish from him and how he wanted him to pay.

Smokey kept his face calm despite his rage. He stared straight ahead, watching Hans out of the corner of his eyes. Hans circled back to face off with Smokey and held the knife again like a swordsman ready for a duel.

"*Your* fish?" Smokey said.

"Yeah, *my* fish, you little thief," Hans said back.

This slur made every hair on the back of Smokey's neck stand straight up. He was a lot of things, but a damn thief he was certainly not. Besides, Smokey would have never borrowed Mr. Wilson's truck or Lorenzo's pistol if it hadn't been for Hans and Frank and the wild-ass goose chase they started. He would have already returned Mr. Wilson's truck, the triangle, and the gun if Hans wasn't a lyin' cheatin' no-good son of a whore.

While all these words and slurs fumed inside Smokey's head, he was keenly aware that he would never talk like that out loud in front of his Ma. His Pa, on the other hand, would not have thought twice about Smokey's cussing.

Smokey stepped towards Hans, who was still gripping the knife. Hans raised the knife to remind Smokey he was the one in charge.

"That was my fish and you know it," Smokey said. He stared at Hans with disdain and held his breath so he could regain his composure.

"I didn't steal no fish. I won it fair and square," Hans said.

Smokey had had enough. He charged at Hans and shoved him backward. He caught Hans off guard, who stumbled and nearly fell back onto the card table. He switched his knife into his other hand and made his way back towards Smokey, intent on cutting him this time to teach him a lesson.

Hans lunged and missed Smokey, and they danced around the living room floor. They circled the tiny space. Hans thrust the knife wildly, barely missing Smokey with the sharp steel blade.

Frank had finished his search around Mr. Wilson's property. There was no sign of the old man nor the boys. Feeling full of frustration, he returned to the miner's house. He was walking across the road when a pickup truck came careening toward him. It slid across the gravel and skidded to a stop just a few feet from hitting Frank. It was Mike, the canoe still strapped to the bed of the truck.

Mike had heard from Big Ma that she saw Smokey pass by with Do What and some other kid a few hours before. Mike had known exactly where they were headed. Mike spotted Frank and leapt out of the truck, headed straight for him. Mike was unsteady as ever on his feet and stumbled forward.

"Where are they?" he shouted.

Frank faced Mike, defiant and angry.

"I said where are they?" Mike shouted as he raised his hands like a boxer getting ready to spar.

Frank matched Mike's stare and stood motionless. He slowly clenched his fist. Mike took a step to the right, and Frank mirrored the step by moving left. They continued to dance around the gravel lot, one waiting for the other to make the first move. Frank wished he had the knife he had given to Hans; it would have ended this altercation right then and there. Mike wished he had grabbed his rifle when he jumped out of the truck. Though it was only a few yards away, he was sure Frank would jump him from behind if he turned back to the truck to get it.

Mike continued to circle, waiting for Frank to make a move.

Inside the house, Smokey and Hans were continuing their own dance around the living room.

Hans lunged towards Smokey. He caught the edge of his shirt and nicked his side. The wound wasn't deep, but Smokey started to bleed, and he had had enough. He was immediately reconnected to the feeling of the cold steel shaft of the concealed pistol.

Smokey was fed up and wild violent thoughts raced in his mind. He reached back and gripped his fingers around the butt of the gun. Smokey had always imagined his ma would see him pictured on the front page of the paper at some point in his life. He just never dreamed it would be his mugshot and he'd go down in history as the "Youngest Murderer of McDowell County."

Hans wielded the knife violently, trying to stab Smokey. Smokey began to stumble backwards. As Hans lunged toward Smokey, his foot broke through the rotten wooden boards of the floor, and he fell clear down to his groin.

Smokey tried to catch his balance and released his grip off the gun as he tumbled back against the card table, upsetting it. The cards went flying through the air and the kerosene lamp crashed down onto the floor.

Smokey kicked the knife from Hans's hands and crouched low, ready to defend himself.

The lantern spilled kerosene all over and ignited into a blaze. Smokey, seeing the flames, snatched the old curtain from the window and tried to snuff it out.

The dry-rotted fabric only added more fuel, and the flames flared up even more.

Hans panicked as he saw the flames crawling toward him. He attempted to pull his leg free from the hole in the floor. Though he struggled and squirmed, he couldn't get enough leverage to yank out his leg. He screamed for help, begging Smokey.

Smokey hated Hans, but he didn't want to watch him burn to death. He grabbed him beneath the arms and attempted to pull him from the floor. With every pull, Hans yelped with pain. His leg was probably broken; any pressure sent him into agony.

The flames roared. They had spread quickly along the floor and up the wall. Smoke filled the house.

"Help me!" cried Hans.

Smokey grabbed Hans's hands, desperately trying to pry him free from the floor. Hans shrieked in agony as Smokey heaved and pulled, but he didn't budge.

Both boys were coughing and gasping for air that was no longer fit to breathe. Smokey stooped down to get face-to-face with Hans. He told him to cover his nose and mouth with his shirt. Then he turned and headed towards the window that they had all used to enter the house.

Hans watched him run away and begged Smokey not to leave him. Smokey didn't even look back at Hans or respond to his cries for help; he turned and jumped out the window into the fresh air outside.

Hans tried to call out for help, but his lungs filled with smoke.

Mike and Frank were still squaring off in the front of the house, oblivious to the smoke that was rising up. The breeze carried the whiffs of smoke in the direction of Mr. Wilson's house.

Mike had tired of this dance with Frank. He ran at Frank, wrapping his arms around his waist in an attempt to take him down. Frank was much stronger, though, and tossed Mike to the gravel.

Mike scrambled to his feet and raised his fists in a boxer stance. Frank lunged at Mike, but Mike stood his ground. When Frank got into range, Mike swung at him, narrowly missing his face.

Mike was a decent boxer, even intoxicated. He had taken up the sport his freshman year before he left to work in the mines. He had natural talent, though he was rusty and weary from not sleeping at night and drinking all morning.

Frank wasn't intimidated but was surprised that Mike had come so close to landing a blow.

As the boys fought, the smoke began to rise more prominently behind them. Hans's brothers were watching from the truck and cheering on their brother, whooping and hollering for him to kick Mike's ass. They were also oblivious to the rising smoke.

Smokey peered back through the window and saw Hans's eyes pleading with him to help as he wrestled and struggled to get free. He heard his calls for help fade into coughs and gasps. Smokey searched the ground outside the window, desperate to find the triangle that he had taken from Mr. Wilson's yard. He found it in a patch of grass, lying beside the metal striker used to ring it.

He held the triangle up high and rang it and rang it as loud as he could. Smoke was billowing out the window now and flames were visible from where he stood. He rang it as if his life depended on it, because he knew that if he didn't, Hans might die.

Mr. Wilson had emerged from his porch, squinting toward the blazing house. Smokey was certain that Mr. Wilson had seen him, so he dropped the triangle and scrambled back through the window. The entire house was filled with smoke, and the flames were climbing up the walls. Hans was still fighting to get his leg free but was now starting to lose consciousness.

Smokey ran to Hans. He tried again to free him from the floorboards.

"Hang on!" he coughed.

Hans raised his head enough to notice that it was Smokey. But his eyes were looking heavy, and he struggled to gasp for even the tiniest amount of oxygen. Smokey coughed and tried to pull Hans free. He was now gasping for air himself, but he was determined to get Hans loose.

The floorboards acted like shackles on Hans's leg. He choked and tried to cover his face with his shirt, but the smoke and flames were filling the room. The once dim space was now ablaze with flames.

Smokey struggled to get leverage because he had needed to kneel to keep below the smoke and rising flames. The pistol fell from his waistband with a thud, but he ignored it and kept on trying to free Hans.

Outside, Frank had managed to wrap his arms around Mike's waist when he lunged at him and tackled him to the ground. His brothers cheered like they were watching a prize fight.

They were all so distracted they didn't see Mr. Wilson. He ran toward the two boys wrestling on the ground. Mr. Wilson was wielding a large ax over his head. The brothers looked in awe. They were amazed that an old man could run like that but terrified that he might take the ax to both of them, like rotted logs waiting to be split.

"Look out!" one of the brothers shouted.

Mr. Wilson ran past the two wrestling boys and made his way up the steps. He smashed his ax against the boards that covered the door. With one strike of the ax, he demolished the boards. He raised the ax up again and struck the door dead center, breaking through the rotting wood. Smoke poured out from the opening. He heaved and swung the ax again and again.

With each strike, the door became weaker. With one final blow, the door splintered wide open and smoke billowed out. Large flames licked the walls.

Both Mike and Frank released each other from their grips and watched in awe and confusion as Mr. Wilson entered the burning house. They saw the flames and smoke but were frozen in terror. Mr. Wilson disappeared into the smoke that was now cascading out of the front door.

Frank, Mike, and Hans's brothers rushed to the door but hesitated to go inside. The smoke formed a giant cloud above the house, and they could see the flames roaring in the living room through the hole where the door used to be.

A horn honked and gravel flew as Lorenzo pulled up, driving Mr. Wilson's truck. Do What and Brent hopped out of the passenger side, and Lorenzo dashed after them.

CHAPTER
10

After lunch, Lorenzo had returned to his office and noticed Mr. Wilson's truck was parked in the alley, which was strange, since he rarely left his house besides to come to get groceries or supplies on occasion. When he got back into his office and opened his desk drawer, Lorenzo discovered his pistol was missing. The only person that knew he had one was Smokey. Lorenzo figured that Smokey must have come to the boarding house for help and had taken the gun to defend his friends.

He locked up the office and found the door to Mr. Wilson's truck unlocked, and the keys in the visor. Lorenzo was worried and headed to Geneva's, where he spoke with Jerome. Jerome mentioned that Smokey had been there earlier in the morning along with Do What and some other boy named Brent. Jerome continued how the boys had showed up there in wet clothes, disheveled, and acting all out of sorts.

It was just enough information for Lorenzo to know beyond any shadow of a doubt that Smokey must be in trouble.

Once Lorenzo suspected trouble, he had sprung into action. He had no time to explain it to Jerome, but Lorenzo had put a plan in place with Smokey a long time ago if he ever found himself in another predicament. Lorenzo had written a note that said, "You owe $1.80," and handed it to Jerome.

"If Smokey shows back up here, be sure to give him this and don't say a word. Smokey will know what to do."

Lorenzo hoped to high heaven that Smokey would remember their secret code. One eighty—go back to where you started. Hopefully Smokey would get the message and return to Brent and Do What's hiding place. Lorenzo was certain it was at the abandoned miner's house.

After giving the note to Jerome, Lorenzo decided to drive the truck back to Northfork to look for Smokey at his usual hideout—the miner's house. As Lorenzo sped toward the house, he spotted Do What and Brent walking on the lower road just down from the entrance to the train tracks. He whistled for their attention and told them to jump into the truck.

Do What and Brent explained to Lorenzo that they had been hiding when they saw Mr. Wilson hollering about his stolen truck. They had climbed out the window and headed back down the tracks once they saw that the train had passed. Lorenzo feared Smokey had really gotten himself into trouble this time.

As he pulled into the gravel driveway of the miner's house, he arrived just in time to see Mr. Wilson stumble out of the front door, dragging Smokey by one arm and carrying a limp body in the other.

Mr. Wilson had made his way into the house and found Smokey still struggling to free a now totally unconscious Hans. Like superman, Mr. Wilson, who was six feet four inches tall, lifted Hans straight up out of the hole and tossed him over his shoulders.

By now, the flames had almost engulfed the entire living room. With the confidence of a firefighter, he grabbed Smokey's arm and led him out the door along with Hans securely in his grip. As they rushed out onto the porch and down the front steps, the entire building went up in flames. The ceiling collapsed with a crash into the spot where Hans and Smokey were trapped just moments before.

Mr. Wilson laid the unconscious Hans on the ground, and Smokey fell to his knees, coughing and gagging from the smoke inhalation. He reached for Hans and passed out before his hand could get to him.

Smokey awoke from what he thought was a dream inside of the small canoe floating on the river. The sun was high overhead, and Do What and Brent were paddling quietly down the river. He wondered how long he had been sleeping. He wasn't sure where they got the other paddle from, since he remembered that they had lost one going down the rapids.

The sun was bright and he struggled to see clearly. He tried to clear his mind by blinking his eyes. He tried to sit up, but someone kept pushing him back down. He was confused and uncertain. Why were Do What and Brent so calm after barely surviving the toughest rapids on the Greenbrier?

His eyes grew heavy and he felt a burning sensation in his chest. He closed his eyes to try to regain focus but felt himself drifting to sleep. He could feel his body lying on solid ground but couldn't seem to get his eyes to open fully. He struggled to wake himself from this strange dream, but each time he felt like his eyes and chest were heavy. He heard Do What's voice calling him.

"Smokey!"

It was muffled, as if he was a hundred yards away. He tried again to wake himself from this strange dream, and this time his eyes flickered open. The strange voices seemed to drift away, and he saw Do What and Brent looking down on him.

"Smokey, are you okay?" Do What asked.

He was kneeling down over him and Brent stood behind him. There was a commotion going on around him, but he couldn't make sense of it. How had everything changed so quickly? He had just been in the canoe, and now he was somewhere on land. He turned his head to the right and saw Mr. Wilson standing over him like a skyscraper in a big city. Suddenly, reality hit him.

His face was covered in soot, and he was breathing heavy, coughing at times. He searched for Hans and was relieved when he spotted him lying on the ground across from him.

Frank hovered over his brother, shouting for Hans to wake up, but Hans lay motionless. Frank slapped his face a few times trying to get him to wake up. Smokey could hear the quiet cries of Hans's brothers and he could see the tears that streamed down Franks face.

Smokey pushed himself up and crawled over to Frank, placing a hand on his shoulder. Frank turned to look at Smokey with desperate eyes.

Smokey motioned for him to let him get closer to Hans. Smokey kneeled over Hans and gently pinched his nose and titled his head back. Smokey took a big breath and placed his lips over Hans's soot covered face. His chest rose and fell as Smokey turned his head to listen for any breath. He breathed again and pushed his air into Hans's lungs. Again his chest rose and fell before collapsing into stillness once again.

"Come on, little buddy," Frank whispered brokenly. "Breathe."

Smokey continued to breathe for Hans. The onlookers stared as Smokey methodically continued to give his breath to Hans, the boy who just moments before had cut his side and tried to kill him. His shirt was covered in ashes and blood, but no one noticed. They were all focused on the breaths of life that Smokey was giving Hans.

Smokey glanced over and locked eyes for a moment with Do What. As tears streamed down Do What's face, he stared intently at Smokey and lifted his hand to his forehead as he'd done many times in the past, making their salute. He believed in Smokey and with the gesture of his hand he assured him not to give up. It was the signal Smokey needed to keep going and believe that a miracle was still possible.

Smokey took one more long breath and with a hushed voiced said, "Breathe, Hans."

With that final breath, Hans choked and coughed and then began to breathe on his own. Frank scooped Hans up off the ground into his arms and held him, weeping. His once tough and angry exterior had melted away.

The sound of a siren could be heard in the distance; it grew louder and louder until the ambulance and the sheriff pulled into the dirt parking lot right where the crowd gathered to watch. The paramedics made their way to Hans. He wasn't completely conscious but was now breathing on his own.

Smokey stepped back and let the medics do their job.

When the sheriff stopped his vehicle, two civilians stepped out of the car: a man and a woman. They were finely dressed and ran to Brent, calling his name. It was Brent's parents. They all hugged and wrapped their arms around their son.

The father grabbed Brent by the arms, looked him in his eyes, and said, "We thought we lost you." He began to sob.

Brent's mother held him to her chest. She didn't seem to notice the dirt being smeared over her picture-perfect outfit. She held her son tightly and wept.

The sheriff got out of the police car and another man exited from the passenger side. He was more of a common looking fellow, dressed in overalls and a conductor's hat. He walked with a cane and limped behind the sheriff as fast as his tired, broken body would allow. He made his way to Hans, Frank, and the brothers. He knelt down and placed his arm around Frank, who hadn't even noticed him until that moment.

Frank turned and recognized that it was his father. His eyes welled up with sorrow. His father leaned in and placed his hand on Hans's face, still not uttering a single word. Hans's eyes flickered open, instinctively as if he sensed his father was there.

The medics gave the father a moment but then urged him to let them get the boy to the hospital. They feared that the smoke might have damaged his lungs, and they needed to give him oxygen to help him recover. They loaded Hans into the ambulance and his father gestured for the rest of the boys to get into the truck. Frank tried to protest, but his father, in a hushed voice, told him not to embarrass him any further. He obliged and walked, head down, towards the truck. He walked past Smokey and Mr. Wilson and then paused, looking back over his shoulder.

"Thanks for getting my brother out of there and saving his life," Frank said.

Mr. Wilson gave a nod in acknowledgment then turned and walked away.

Smokey looked down at his soot and blood-soaked shirt for a second then raised his head and locked eyes with Frank. "I'm glad he's okay. You would have done the same," he said.

Frank continued to the pickup and got into the passenger side while the rest of the brothers climbed in back of the truck.

Hans's father limped over to Brent and his family, shaking their hands and apologizing for the trouble his sons had caused. He knew that they could press charges and have Frank, who was eighteen, arrested for kidnapping. They had already discussed why his boys were upset and about the accident that led to his injuries and losing his job as a coal miner.

Brent's father was a fair and decent man. Though he was no longer at the mines, he was upset with how the mining company had treated the accident. It bothered him that there had not been any pension or compensation for the man's injuries. On the ride down, he had offered Hans's father a job supervising the miner equipment shop. Brent's father explained that he had been the CEO of the shop for many years and could use a good man on the job.

Hans's father turned to head to the pickup truck and stopped to acknowledge Smokey and Mr. Wilson. He reached out his hand to thank them for saving his boy's life. Smokey and Mr. Wilson shook hands with him but said nothing, just nodded their heads.

Earlier in the day, when Lorenzo had met Hans and Frank at his office, he knew something was wrong. They were not from Cinder Bottom, or anywhere down in the County, so he went immediately to Jerome, who was working in the kitchen at Geneva's restaurant. He figured if they were looking for Smokey, they were looking for trouble—it followed him everywhere.

On his way to the restaurant, he had bumped into Ray, the owner of the local grocery store, who had just made his way back from Bluefield, the largest city in the southern part of West Virginia. Ray made weekly runs there back and forth to get supplies. Bluefield was also where he got the local paper. That morning, he had learned that a boy had gone missing just across the state line in Virginia and that the authorities suspected foul play.

Connecting the dots, Lorenzo had contacted the sheriff to tell him that he knew where the missing boy might be. Brent's parents had received a call from the sheriff in Cinder Bottom to let them know of the lead they had. According to Lorenzo, Hans's father approached Brent's family to tell them that he thought that his boys might be involved. The boys had been missing.

They had all made their way to Cinder Bottom, and that's how they knew where they were. A neighbor had called the fire department when they heard the distressful ringing of the triangle and saw the smoke rising from the abandoned building.

The firemen rushed around, trying to put out the flames that engulfed the entire house. There was no chance of saving the dwelling. It was like a pile of kindling that had been soaked in kerosene and then lit. Their only hope was to prevent the fire from spreading to the surrounding area.

Mike, Do What, and Lorenzo watched them extinguish what was left of the flames. Smokey made his way around to the other side of the property where he discovered Mr. Wilson, who was clutching the iron triangle to his chest.

"Mr. Wilson, sir," Smokey said in a calm but respectful voice. He had never once said a word to the man. "I'm sorry I stole your triangle and your truck . . . well, borrowed really."

Mr. Wilson stood there in contemplation and looked down at him. He gazed into his eyes that welled up with tears.

"Thank you, young man," Mr. Wilson said as he held the triangle even tighter to his chest. "You reminded me that I had a reason to live." He patted Smokey on the shoulder and grinned. "The next time you need to borrow my truck, just ask."

He left Smokey and headed towards his house. Smokey watched him hang the triangle back in its place and disappear inside.

Smokey walked back towards the sheriff and was met by Brent and his family.

"This is Smokey. He's the one who saved my life," Brent said. "And that's Do What. They're my friends!"

His parents reached out their hands to thank them both. Brent's father reached into his back pocket to retrieve his billfold, but Smokey held his hands up.

"No, sir, I can't take any money," Smokey said. Do What was also shaking his head in protest.

"We have to do something to thank you for rescuing our son," Brent's mother said.

Do What and Smokey looked at each other and shrugged. Though they lost their hideout and the band of brothers would be upset that they no longer could host Friday nights playing cards, they would soon find other things to keep their interest.

With the fire extinguished, Lorenzo and the sheriff drove Brent and his parents back to town, and Do What and Mike gave Smokey a ride home. He knew he would spend the rest of the afternoon trying to explain to his mother why he was so filthy, covered in soot, and blood.

All Smokey had wanted was to float the river and do a little fishing, but life has a way of giving you something different from what you expect.

It was a perfect day to float the river. Do What was waiting for Smokey to pick him up at the same spot as the last time they planned to fish. Smokey pulled up alongside Do What, whose head was buried in a *National Geographic* as usual. He barely noticed the truck pull up. Smokey was driving Mr. Wilson's truck, and strapped in the bed was a brand-new canoe with two beautiful wooden paddles.

Do What and Smokey had refused to accept any money from Brent's parents, but the next week, a truck delivered a brand-new, top-of-the-line sport canoe to Smokey's house. He didn't want to accept it because he knew he would have to give it to Mike for ruining the one they had destroyed. But to their surprise, Mike told them to keep it.

Do What jumped into the cab of the truck, and they made their way down the road. Smokey drove for over an hour, and they rode side by side without the need to speak.

They decided to park and float a short way down to the same spot where they had caught the infamous giant smallmouth bass that Hans had stolen from them. Smokey knew it would be a long shot to come across the fish again. He figured it would be nowhere to be found, but they decided to enjoy the calm morning just the same.

He helped Do What bait his hook with a meaty hellgrammite, and they cast their lines into the water. The sun was warm, but it was still early and barely making its way above the tree line.

Smokey thought about the kidnapping in the cabin, the rapids and Brent almost drowning, the gun shot into the gravel, the truck sliding over the hill to miss the buck, the miner's house, the knife fight with Hans, the fire, Mr. Wilson rescuing Hans from the flames, and the breath of life given so that Hans could live. So many events in just one day. He could hardly believe it was real, but things like this always seemed to happen to Smokey. He wanted a cigarette but had decided that he needed to quit. After sucking in so much smoke rescuing Hans, he was ready to put all of that behind him.

He relaxed into a deeper meditative state, enjoying the peace and quiet that he had so desperately longed for just a few weeks before. He rested the pole between his legs and let the sun warm his face. He closed his eyes and remembered how much he loved fishing, not just for the fish, but because it was one place he felt like he belonged. It was something about the river and the calmness of nature.

Do What had set his pole down as well and was deep into his magazine once again, telling Smokey about the amazing ruins of the ancient Mayans.

Smokey smiled. Things seemed to be back to normal.

He rested his pole in his right hand, leaned back, and closed his eyes again. The canoe made its way down the peaceful river and the sunlight danced across the water. The wind was still, and everything felt just right. In Smokey's eyes, everything was picture perfect.

Suddenly, the pole between his legs nearly leapt from his grip into the water. He caught it just before it plunged into the river. He grabbed the pole and began to reel it in. There was a fish on the end, no doubt, and it was big.

Smokey fought hard to pull the line in. Each crank of the shaft seemed harder than the last.

"Holy smokes, it's a big one!" Do What yelled, almost tipping the canoe over.

"Sit down, Do What!" Smokey hollered. He was pulling the pole and reeling with all his might. He would have done a better job if he was standing, but the canoe would tip over with the force of the fish's fight. He continued to reel in the line, and the canoe seemed to be pulled in the direction of the fish. This was not a snagged line; this was a fish that was not giving in at all.

Do What whooped and hollered for Smokey to get that fish. He reeled and reeled. But the fish kept tugging and pulling. He pulled with all his might, but knew he had to be careful or the fish might break free from the hook.

Do What stood again and pointed.

"Look!" he shouted.

It was the prized fish they had lost to Hans. The sun hit it just right, and they could see the size of this enormous smallmouth bass.

Smokey was determined to catch him. He coaxed it closer and closer to the boat where Do What stood with the net, teetering the canoe to and fro, almost tipping them over yet again. Soon the fish was within five feet of the canoe, and Smokey could feel the victory of catching the largest fish in the Greenbrier River for the second time. This time, he would be the hero, one who caught the prize fish.

Smokey slowed his reeling to make sure not to spook the fish that was already getting tired. It would use all of its remaining energy to break free if it had the chance. The last moment was the most critical.

When the fish was at the boat, Smokey gave one last pull and reeled the enormous fish out of the water. Do What caught him with the net, and it nearly pulled him over the side of the canoe. The net was too small to contain it.

Do What set the fish in the bottom of the canoe, and it flipped and struggled to get free from the net. The boys let out a loud cheer. They had done it! They had caught the prized fish! They gave each other high fives and celebrated, almost capsizing the canoe.

They both sat and stared at the huge fish, whose flesh showed many scars and hooks still imbedded deep in its sides from times where it had been hooked but somehow got away.

Smokey and Do What stared at the enormous fish and stood in awe of its size and beauty. It was the kind of fish that was stuffed and hung in a cabin or lodge. The kind of fish that was talked about around campfires and became legendary in the small towns of West Virginia.

Smokey bent over the beautiful fish and pinned him down with his weight as he grabbed the pliers to remove the hook from his mouth. The fish squirmed and almost flipped Smokey from the canoe. He was able to get the hook free and sat back on the small seat staring at the fish. He thought about how hard the last trip down the river had been for him and Do What and realized that this fish had survived more than one crazy fight on this river. Something in him felt strange and melancholy; it wasn't pity but reverence for a fish that had lived so long and survived so many attempts to be a prize.

Smokey, without saying anything, reached into the net, took the fish by the gills, and returned it to the water. The fish flipped and turned when it hit the water and took off into the shadows of the river. Do What looked at him in wonder.

"Why did you let him go?" Do What asked.

"He deserves to live," Smokey said.

With that, he placed more bait on his hook and cast his line into the water. Do What shrugged and did the same.

They sat on the river for a few more hours. They never discussed the fish again. Not then, not ever.

They drove home in silence, except for the occasional outburst of excitement from Do What's discovery in his magazine of some exotic place.

Smokey smiled and felt the comfort of having a friend that understood him. It was more than most could ever want, the end of the best day of his life.

SMOKEY AND DO WHAT'S
ADVENTURES IN CINDER BOTTOM
DON'T STOP HERE!

HERE'S AN EXCLUSIVE
SNEAK PEEK AT BOOK 3:

A PLACE CALLED HOME

Big Ma sat on the oversized wooden rocking chair on the back porch of the "house," waiting for Raymond to arrive. The cool air that filled the hills and hollers of Southern West Virginia were as common as fireflies at night.

Big Ma's "house" was a simple structure, a cinder block home with ample open space in the back that served as the bar and gathering area of the evening patrons. During the late evenings, the house became a place for menfolk to gather, socialize, and drink, and as the night wore on, it was a place to lay with women.

A brothel is a quiet, still place in the early mornings. Ma waited as she always did on Sunday for Raymond to arrive. Big Ma, as she was called, was given the name of Charlene Meredith Lewis at birth, but she despised that name now, and unless there was an official reason to use it, she went by the name Big Ma.

She was a large sturdy woman whose dark eyes and taut black skin gave her the presence of a woman not to be bothered, especially not on a warm day like today. She sat rocking ever so slightly not to soothe herself but to keep pace with the minute hand of a clock as if she were keeping time with each motion. She didn't like to be kept waiting, and at any minute she would get up and walk back in if he didn't arrive.

She was patient with many things but not with anyone who would keep her waiting. She was not one to wait for any man, especially not today. She needed to get to Bluefield, West Virginia by 10 a.m. and was not interested in being late.

The house was quiet now, though just seven hours before, it had been bustling with patrons, young women, and the musty smell of moonshine and beer—cheap beer, the only kind served in Cinder Bottom. Like most weekend nights, the last call was just a formality to signal to the men that gathered that they were nearly out of liquor. That's when some men showed up looking for the girls that were waiting for their opportunity, as Big Ma would call it, to make their living.

The girls that came to Big Ma's place often were barely eighteen and fled some worse situation back home. No one came to Cinder Bottom by mistake. They came to look for something, something to ease their mind, free them or help them escape the life they had.

Though Cinder Bottom had been a red-light district for nearly sixty years, it was still as small and unassuming as it had been in the beginning, though the modern world eventually found its way there. It looked frozen at the turn of the century, the sound of the 1950s radio could be heard in the distance with the crooning of the likes of Elvis Presley, Ella Fitzgerald, and Hank Williams.

Big Ma didn't listen to music unless there were others around. She loved music, and she had a beautiful voice in her youth and sang solos in her church choir in Shelby County, Tennessee. She was stunning, and her strong facial features were attributed to her father's Chickasaw blood. Her family had worked as sharecroppers in the cotton fields and lived in the area for nearly two hundred years.

She was raised by her grandfather, who was a preacher and had raised her in the church along with her seven brothers and sisters, but she was seen as the prize of the family on account of her beautiful voice. Her grandfather would often take her with him on his revival trips along the Mississippi River Valley to sing for the congregations and spiritual revivals that he would visit.

She always felt special when she was with her "Pappi," as she called her grandfather. He would parade her around the squares of the small towns and would treat her to a cold pop when she had finished her Sunday performance. He called her singing "the voice of God," and he reminded her how special she was even as a nine-year-old girl.

Charlene would feel uncomfortable with too much attention, except from her Pappi. From him, she wanted as much attention as he would allow. He would often confide in her that as she grew older that her beauty was matching her voice. He had sat her on his lap from a little age and sang to her when she was a child. He made her feel special and gave her more attention than her siblings and other grandchildren. To him, those others weren't as special as she was.

As she grew older, she would still long to sit on her Pappi's lap and when there was no one around he would invite her to sit on his knee. He would caress her beautiful hair and rub her back and ask her to sing. His gentle touches had been reassurance to Charlene, since her father had left her ma when she was just three years old.

Charlene felt that she didn't matter much in her family, and her grandfather was the only one who really cared about her. The other family members resented the attention she received, and her siblings didn't like that she often was not required to do chores around the house. Her pappi said that she was gonna bring them all a lot of opportunity one day and they needed to appreciate her gift.

Though her grandfather's approval was what she craved more than anything, she started to sense his uneasiness with Charlene's blossoming figure, and he didn't like the attention that many men gave her beyond her brilliant voice. He told her that she was his and they couldn't have her. There was part of her that loved the attention and part of it that made her feel uneasy and more like a prop in a show than a young girl.

On one particular trip when she was twelve years old, just one week from her thirteenth birthday, her grandfather invited Charlene to visit a small congregation on the border of Kentucky to sing for a special guest named Samuel Williams, the deacon of a prominent church in Atlanta.

Her grandfather had wanted to impress the deacon with his granddaughter's beautiful voice, which also matched her blossoming physical beauty. She was tall for her age and was beginning to transition from a child to a young woman.

The deacon had a nice piece of land that he might help her grandfather acquire so they could stop being sharecroppers and actually own their own land. Her Pappi had told her to do whatever she could to please

Mr. Williams and to win his favor. Charlene loved her grandfather and always wanted to live up to his expectations and learned every song he requested and sang with her whole heart.

On the Sunday that they visited, she sang the most beautiful version of the song "His Eye Is on the Sparrow." The congregation was moved, and so was deacon Williams, so much so that he invited her grandfather to lunch at his hotel.

In the lobby after the service, Pappi and Deacon Williams exchanged private words while Charlene waited near the entrance of the all-black establishment. The deacon and her grandfather chatted for a bit, glancing occasionally back at her. Her grandfather returned to Charlene and gestured for her to go with Deacon Williams, who wanted to thank her personally for her lovely performance.

She was a shy girl, though when she sang her timidity vanished and her beautiful angelic voice filled any church or hall where she sang. She shuffled her feet as she made her way to the deacon. Her grandfather said he would be waiting for her just outside. She looked over her shoulder at her grandfather, who gestured for her to continue. She made her way to Deacon Williams, and he reached out his hand to her elbow to escort her toward the hotel elevators. Charlene searched for her grandfather and saw him walking out of the hotel entrance. She stopped and turned from Deacon Williams, who assured her that she would be safe with him. Her grandfather vanished out the front door.

Deacon Williams told Charlene as he led her into the elevator how much he loved her singing and praised her beautiful skin and hair. The elevator doors opened, and he stepped in and motioned for her to follow him. Though she was hesitant, she remembered that her grandfather said to do whatever pleased Mr. Williams, so she stepped inside reluctantly.

When the elevator closed and there was no sign of her grandfather, Charlene knew that things in her life were not as they seemed. She had had a relatively calm ordinary life. Though her grandparents didn't have much time for her with six other children to look after she always felt taken care of and watched over, especially by her grandfather, she trusted her Pappi.

Deacon Williams escorted Charlene out of the elevator and to the door of his hotel room. He fumbled with the keys, and Charlene took a series of small steps backward when he finally opened the door and gestured for her to enter. Charlene felt the blood run to her face as she realized that the deacon was not interested in thanking her for her performance but wanted to take advantage of her blossoming beauty.

When she backed away, the deacon grabbed her arm forcefully and yet his words conveyed a more luring tone.

"Don't you worry Ms. Charlene," the deacon said gently. "I won't bite."

The sinister sound of his voice petrified Charlene, and she was a statue as he tried to pull her closer to the door. When she still refused, the deacon calmly moved the hair from her face and placed his hand on her shoulder.

"Now, you don't want to make your grandpa upset do you?" he said.

She glared at him, trying to rationalize his behavior as if perhaps she was just interpreting the situation incorrectly. Maybe she had let her imagination run wild and there was nothing to be worried about. Her grandfather would never put her in a situation that would cause her any harm, she was certain of that. But still, she felt uneasy and was reluctant to enter the room. Perhaps he just wanted to hear her sing in private so that he could praise her for her beautiful voice?

The bell for the elevator chimed, and a sweet older black woman emerged wearing a beautiful blue dress and a Sunday hat to match. She stared oddly at them, but the deacon politely removed his hat and wished her a good afternoon, still holding one hand on Charlene's shoulder. She glanced back once over her shoulder but disappeared around the corner as she made her way to her room.

The hall was long and the red carpet accentuated the cream color walls that were covered in intricate woodwork. The hotel was for blacks only, but it was nice and held a certain amount of charm.

Deacon Williams urged Charlene to please enter the room, that he just wanted to talk, though she stood at the door in protest. His pleading was beginning to wear her down, and before she knew what she was doing, she stepped through the doorway of the deacon's room. The deacon was older than her grandfather. Charlene's grandmother had always instructed her to be polite, proper, and respectful to her elders.

Once inside, he quickly closed and locked the door and then he offered Charlene a cold cola that he had on ice in his room. She had been wanting one since her grandfather had always bought one for her on Sundays after her solos. She figured that there would be no harm in having a cold cola. He handed her the bottle that was still dripping with sweat from being chilled.

"Careful now, it's wet," he said while handing her his handkerchief that was worn thin and yellow from age from his pocket to keep the water off her hand.

She slowly brought the bottle to her mouth and drank, keeping her eyes on the deacon as she swallowed the delicious cold cola. It wasn't the familiar Coke that her grandfather bought, her but was refreshing nonetheless.

After three long drinks, he took the bottle from her hand placed it on the dresser, and began to make his way closer to her, staring at her intently.

"You have beautiful eyes, Ms. Charlene," he said as he held her hand. She fidgeted to escape his grip, but his hand clasped tightly around her wrist. He pulled her close and tried to kiss her. She instinctively pulled away and tried to free her arm from his grip. He was older but still much stronger than she was. With her free arm, she pushed him away defending her lips from his unwanted advance.

"Now come on, Ms. Charlene. Let's have a kiss," he said as he pulled her into his body. "Such a pretty girl wants to be kissed," he insisted.

Charlene struggled to free herself, and he forced her back. She collapsed onto the bed, nearly hitting her head on the dresser where the cola bottle rocked back and forth.

"No!" she shouted as she fought to get her hands free from his grip.

He lowered himself onto her and his heavy breath neared her lips. She squirmed to avoid his kiss and he managed to land a kiss on her cheek. With his free hand, he reached down towards her dress slowly bringing his hand up her thigh.

"Stop!" she protested, but he did not and when his hand reached her underpants, her struggle began to become spasmatic and she kicked and wiggled beneath his heavy body. With her free hand, she pushed his face from hers and forced his hand away.

She felt his body pressing against hers and wanted to call for her grandfather, but no words came out. She felt powerless for a moment but reached back and clasped the nearly full cola bottle in her hand and crashed it down on the deacon's head with one powerful blow to his temple.

The deacon slumped off her body and made a thud on the hotel room floor. Charlene gasped as she felt the air from holding her breath return to her body. She leapt from the bed, ran for the door, and bolted down the hallway to the exit sign over the stairs. She made her way down four flights of stairs, not even certain if she had touched a single step.

When she burst into the lobby, the eyes of the hotel's guests waiting to check in turned to see this young girl, disheveled panting as she ran towards the door of the hotel lobby, grateful that her grandfather would be waiting for her. She burst into the daylight feeling like she had just escaped prison, searching for her grandfather, but there was no sign of him. He was not waiting just outside of the hotel as he had told her.

"Where are you," she said to herself, panting trying to catch her breath but had no idea where he could be. She figured he might be waiting at the car and made her way back to the parking spot where they had left it earlier, but he wasn't there.

She began to panic, thinking that deacon Williams would be waking up soon and discover that she wasn't there and start to search for her. She didn't want to be anywhere near the hotel so she began to run. She ran down the main road as far as she could until she nearly collapsed, but she pressed on and walked until she could walk no more.

TO OUR DAD, SMOKEY,

There are so many things I could write about our dad, Smokey, and how much he inspired us to write these stories. His passion for storytelling and his belief in the importance of life and love were the driving forces behind this book. We are forever grateful for his influence and the stories he shared with us.

Dad gave us a glimpse into what life was like when he grew up in the hollers of Northfork, West Virginia. The stories and his perspective were so unique of the communities in that part of Appalachia. Throughout his life, he watched the area rise and fall economically and socially. It's like Dad got to see it toward the high points and also the big decline.

He grew up near a red-light district named Cinder Bottom, in a place misunderstood by most of the world outside of McDowell County. Dad saw the good in people and also got to see the wild side of coal mining communities where corruption, gambling, and prostitution were kept in business for decades in a remote and hidden place in the mountains of southern West Virginia.

ABOUT THE AUTHORS

STEVE VANNOY was born to Curtis "Smokey" and Peggy Vannoy, and he was raised in Bluefield, West Virginia. As a grandson, nephew, and cousin of several coal miners throughout Appalachia, Steve gained a unique perspective into the history of McDowell  County, where both of his parents were born and raised. His love of West Virginia and its rich history from an early age led him to become a winner of the "Golden Horseshoe" award. Steve's mission in writing these stories is to preserve the life and community light on the place called home tucked in between the hills and hollows of southern West Virginia.

Trained as an industrial engineer at West Virginia University, Steve worked in various industries across the state. He is the cofounder of an award-winning publishing company and spends his time with his partner, his family, and their two adorable pups.

AZUL TERRONEZ is a *Wall Street Journal* and *USA Today* bestselling author. His TEDx talk, *What Makes a Good Teacher Great*, has been viewed over 4 million times.

This is his second novel, and he is proud to share his partner's love for West Virginia.

He spends his time writing books, coaching authors, and telling stories from the stage. He splits his time between Santa Cruz, California, and Portugal. When not writing, he is spending time with his family and playing with his rambunctious dogs.

If you enjoyed Smokey and Do What's
second Adventure in Cinder Bottom,
please leave a **REVIEW** on Amazon.

Follow along as their story continues at

CINDERBOTTOM.COM

Thank you!

www.ingramcontent.com/pod-product-compliance
Lightning Source LLC
Chambersburg PA
CBHW030332030726
47499CB00003B/742